A shock ▓▓▓▓▓▓
of her f▓ ▓▓▓▓▓▓
almost like excitement.

She dropped the necklace to the table and discovered she was breathing hard, as if she'd run here instead of tottering on ridiculously high heels.

Still he said nothing, just watched her with eyes that glowed with an inner fire.

No time for second thoughts. She'd committed herself. Head up, back straight, she paced towards him. He didn't move except to tilt his head, the better to watch her.

Had he enjoyed this power play. She sensed it even though his face remained granite hard.

He been so sure she'd come to him?

Of course he had. He held all the cards.

ANNIE WEST discovered romance early—her childhood best friend's house was an unending store of Harlequin® books—and she's been addicted ever since. Fortunately she found her own real-life romantic hero while studying at university, and married him. After gaining (despite the distraction) an honors classics degree, Annie took a job in the public service. For years she wrote and redrafted and revised: government plans, letters for cabinet ministers and reports for parliament. Checking the text of a novel is so much more fun! Annie started to write romance when she took leave to spend time with her children. Between school activities she produced her first novel. At the same time she discovered Romance Writers of Australia. Since then she's been active in RWAus writers' groups and competitions. She attends annual conferences, and loves the support she gets from so many other writers. Her first Harlequin novel came out in 2005.

Annie lives with her hero (still the same one) and her children at Lake Macquarie, north of Sydney, and spends her time fantasizing about gorgeous men and their love lives. It's hard work, but she has no regrets!

Annie loves to hear from readers. You can contact her via her website, www.annie-west.com or at annie@annie-west.com.

Books by Annie West

Harlequin Presents® Extra
#137—*Protected by the Prince*

Harlequin Presents®
#3010—*Prince of Scandal*

All backlist available in ebook.

THE SAVAKIS MERGER
ANNIE WEST

~ Tall, Dark and Dangerously Sexy ~

Harlequin®

TORONTO NEW YORK LONDON
AMSTERDAM PARIS SYDNEY HAMBURG
STOCKHOLM ATHENS TOKYO MILAN MADRID
PRAGUE WARSAW BUDAPEST AUCKLAND

Recycling programs
for this product may
not exist in your area.

ISBN-13: 978-0-373-52838-7

THE SAVAKIS MERGER

First North American Publication 2011

THE SAVAKIS MERGER

To two lovely ladies:
Marilyn and Lee.
Thank you for all your support!

CHAPTER ONE

CALLIE's heart thundered in her ears, muting the sound of their hoarse breathing. Hers and his, mingled together.

Aftershocks shuddered through her. Light flickered behind her closed lids, remnants of the white-hot ecstasy that had exploded through her moments ago. An ecstasy she'd never before experienced.

Who could have known?

She dragged in a breath and inhaled his spicy scent. Clean masculine sweat, musky skin and something indefinable that made her want to burrow closer into his bare shoulder.

She nuzzled his damp skin and was rewarded with a rumble of approval deep in the wide chest that cushioned her. One large hand slid gently over her hip, long fingers caressing her bare flesh, pulling her closer to his hot, slick body so she lay half across him.

Callie's breath puffed out in a sigh of astonished bliss. He was strong, tender and generous.

Everything she'd never had from a man.

Everything she'd learned not to expect.

He'd taken her to paradise. Teased and pleasured her until reality shattered in a conflagration of sheer bliss.

She'd never known such intense joy as when she'd soared to ecstasy in his arms. She'd always be grateful for the gift he'd given her today. The shared pleasure that connected her, however briefly, to him. That sense of linkage, even more than the physical delight, warmed her to the core.

She'd felt alone for so long.

From the moment she'd seen him row his dinghy from the gracious old yacht, his wide shoulders gleaming bare and golden in the sun, she'd sensed something different about him. Something special. He epitomised a masculinity so perfect it had sucked the breath from her chest.

She, Callie Manolis, who hadn't looked at a man with desire in seven years! Who'd thought she never would again.

For days she'd tried to ignore the stranger who invaded the seclusion of this private beach. Invaded her refuge. Each morning as she lay under the pine trees, spent from swimming, she attempted to focus on her book. But inevitably her gaze strayed to where he pottered on deck, fished, or swam in the clear waters of the tiny bay.

Even with her eyes shut she'd been aware of him. As he'd been of her.

Had he really needed to ask the way to the track for the nearest village? The sizzling gleam in his eyes told her he hadn't. But for once Callie had warmed to that wholly male glint of appreciation. It hadn't repelled or annoyed her.

He looked the way she felt when she saw him.

Ensnared by his dark, dark eyes, Callie had been like a swimmer adrift on the Aegean, cut off from reality. From her future plans, the pain of the past, even her distrust of men. What did trust matter in the face of this potent attraction? It was extraordinary yet stunningly simple.

Her lips curved against his skin. She couldn't resist the temptation to press a kiss there, tasting his salt tang. A sound between a growl and a purr vibrated from his throat, exactly matching her own sense of lazy triumph.

Perhaps sexual abstinence made this sudden passion so exhilarating. She was twenty-five and he was her second lover. Perhaps that was why...

Thought clogged as his hand moved splay-fingered down

her leg. It circled, light as a wind-blown leaf, slipping between their bodies to caress her sensitive inner thigh.

Callie sucked in an astonished breath as the tingling started again deep inside. A jolt of desire pierced her, shocking her to full awareness in an instant.

Heat radiated from his touch as his hand strayed to the place where need had pulsed a short time ago. She gasped as he stroked her, tenderly yet deliberately. Stunned, she felt a shimmer of excitement ripple through her sated body like a rising tide.

'You like that?' There was lazy satisfaction in his deep voice. And a knowledge that told her he knew *exactly* how much she craved his touch.

He understood her reactions better than she. Callie was a novice at this but even a woman so inexperienced recognised a master of the sensual arts.

She flattened her hands on his chest and pushed herself up so she could look down into his face.

A smile lingered on his sensuous lips and his glittering eyes flashed an invitation. His unruly black hair flopped over his brow, in gorgeous disarray after she'd clutched it. Her gaze strayed past his solid jaw to the strong column of his throat. To the reddened patch on his neck.

Was that a love bite? She'd marked him with her teeth? Surely she hadn't been so wild.

'We can't,' she blurted out. 'Not again.'

One sleek black brow rose and he bestowed a slow confident smile that sent a buzz of pleasure through her.

'I wouldn't be too sure of that, little one.'

His questing fingers moved and her body trembled.

Automatically she clamped her fingers around his wrist, intending to drag his hand away. She needed to think. But she couldn't shift him. His arm was all hard bone and muscled strength. His touch was bliss.

'Yes,' he whispered, his gaze fixed on her with searing intensity. 'Hold me while I touch you.'

Callie's eyes widened at his deliberate eroticism. Her heart leapt. The melting warmth between her legs belied her instinctive denial and she squirmed.

After their desperate lovemaking this should be impossible. Yet the feel of his sinewed hand moving beneath hers was... exciting. As was the burgeoning strength of his arousal against her thighs.

'No.' Her voice was breathless. She squeezed her eyes shut, trying to claim control of her wayward body. 'I have to go. I have to—'

'Shh, *glikia mou*,' he murmured in that seductive, black-velvet voice. He withdrew his hand to cup her face with callused fingers. He stroked the erogenous zone at the corner of her mouth she hadn't known existed till today. 'Relax and enjoy. There's no rush. Nothing more important than this.'

His hand slid to the back of her head and he pulled her inexorably down to meet his mouth. The kiss was long, languorous and seductive. Callie's resistance seeped away like sea water through sand. Her bones melted as her lips opened and he ravaged her mouth with sweet possessiveness.

How could anything so unprecedented feel so right?

'You can leave later,' he murmured against her lips, each word a caress. 'Afterwards.'

Afterwards. The word circled in Callie's hazy brain then disintegrated as she kissed him back. The remnants of self-control dissolved in the heat of rising passion.

It was oh-so-easy to give herself up to the luxury of his expert seduction. To throw away a lifetime's caution and live for the moment. To forget the real world and the harsh lessons she'd learned there. Just for a little longer.

Madness.

That was what it had been, Callie decided as she stood before the mirror in her guest room. Nothing else could explain the way she'd allowed herself to be seduced.

No, not *allowed*. She'd encouraged him, eager for the feel

of his tall, muscular body against hers. Impatient to pursue the sensual promise she'd read in his eyes. Eager for the sort of loving she'd never had, and now, to her stunned delight, had experienced for the first time.

With a stranger.

Her eyes rounded and a shudder rippled through her at the thought of what she'd done. She, the woman the tabloids had once dubbed the Snow Queen, had given herself to a complete stranger in passionate abandon! Not once. Nor twice. But three times, in heart-stopping succession.

Shock and shame flooded her as she remembered in exquisite detail.

Given herself! She grimaced at her reflection. She hadn't even had the grace to be embarrassed that he carried condoms when he'd come ashore today. All she'd felt was relief.

He had a swimmer's body, broad shoulders, slim hips, with long muscled limbs and the easy stride of a man at ease with his strength. The sort of body she'd seen on beaches at home in Australia a lifetime ago. Not what she'd expect on a tiny island off the tourist trail in northern Greece.

She knew gorgeous men. They left her unmoved. Their charm and good looks had never quickened her pulse.

The gossips had been disappointed as for six years she'd remained loyal to her much older husband.

Even the fact that her husband had desired her only as a possession to display and jealously guard hadn't driven her to seek consolation elsewhere. Alkis had been impotent and Callie had buried her libido as well as her emotions during their sterile, unhappy marriage. More, his sick jealousy and frightening outbursts ensured she kept men at a distance. She'd learned to brush off the importunate ones with a cool grace that had become her hallmark.

Never had she felt this fiery yearning when she looked at a man. Until today, just hours ago in the deserted private cove of her uncle's estate.

It had been a momentary insanity, brought on by worry for

her aunt's health and stress from this duty holiday under her uncle's roof. By the release of unbearable tension after those dreadful last months with Alkis.

By a lifetime of being what her aunt would describe as a 'good girl', doing what was expected.

Callie's lips quirked in a humourless smile as she met her gaze in the mirror. She didn't look like a good girl now.

She'd done as her uncle insisted, donning a full-length gown, totally over-the-top for a family dinner. She'd piled her hair up and wore the flashy diamond pendant and bracelet set that was all she had left of Alkis' gifts.

But the formal clothes didn't conceal the change in her.

There was high colour in her cheeks, her eyes sparkled overbright, her lips were plump as if kissed long and hard by an expert. And that look of secret satisfaction surely must betray her.

She should be mortified by what she'd done.

Yet, staring at the stranger in the glass, she knew an overpowering urge to flee. To forget the stuffy dinner her uncle had organised and race barefoot to the beach and find her stranger.

Her lover.

The man whose name she didn't even know.

But she could never do that. Callie had been trained too well. Ruthlessly she subdued the renegade impulse to ignore a lifetime's lessons and run to the man with whom she'd shared her yearning and her inner self.

She'd had her single afternoon of madness. Now it was over and she had to forget him before he swept away all her desperately won defences.

'I want you girls to make a special effort tonight.' Uncle Aristides turned the statement into a threat. He waggled a warning finger at his daughter, standing beside Callie. 'Especially you, Angela. Your mother's unwell again, so you'll stand in for her.' He spoke disapprovingly, as though Aunt Desma had planned to be ill.

Seeing the scowl wedge between her uncle's beetling brows and the miserable look on Angela's face, Callie swallowed a pithy retort. It would be her docile cousin who'd pay if Callie made her uncle angry.

'The evening will be perfect, Uncle. I've checked with the staff. The meal looks superb and the best vintage champagne is on ice. I'm sure your guest will be impressed.'

Her uncle was even more touchy than usual, lashing out furiously at any perceived problem. Poor Angela was already a bundle of nerves, anticipating an explosion.

'I hope so,' her uncle boomed. 'We have an important visitor tonight.' He emphasised the point with a wave of his hand. 'A *very* important guest.'

Callie's stomach sank with foreboding. What *did* he have planned? This was more than a family celebration for her twenty-fifth birthday. Diamonds and designer gowns weren't usual attire, even in this house where oppressive formality was the norm. He was up to something.

His eyes strayed again to Angela and Callie's curiosity twisted into a stab of anxiety. She knew exactly how ruthless her uncle could be, and how devious.

'Don't forget what I said, Angela,' he barked.

Angela's face paled. 'Yes, father.' At eighteen she had none of her father's brash confidence. Callie knew she found it a chore mixing among her father's associates.

Callie stepped forward. 'Tonight will be a success, Uncle. Don't worry, we'll see to it.'

If she had to dredge up every last ounce of patience to smile and listen to one of his cronies bore on about the iniquities of the government or the flaws of the younger generation, she'd do it. Anything to prevent an angry outburst that would force Angela further into her shell.

Aristides Manolis looked Callie up and down as if seeking to find fault. But six years of marriage to a rich man, of mixing in glamorous society, had given her the gloss to shine in any surroundings. And the experience to handle any social situation.

Dinner for four, even with the most demanding, querulous guest, would be no problem at all.

'You will be our hostess,' he said. 'But I don't want Angela fading into the background as she usually does.'

Callie found herself nodding in unison with Angela. She'd only been in this house five days and already she felt the old yoke of submission settling on her shoulders.

Could it really be just hours ago she'd lain naked in the arms of a man? Brazen enough to have sex with him in a secluded grove of pines by the beach?

As soon as her uncle strode from the room, Callie reached for her cousin's hand. It was cold.

'It'll be OK, Angela. I'm here with you.'

Trembling fingers squeezed hers and she felt her cousin's desperation. Then Angela pulled away, head up, back straight, the picture of elegant composure, as expected of the Manolis girls.

It was something the women in her family learned early. To conceal emotion. To appear calm and agreeable, an ornament and an asset to the right man.

The right man. Callie repressed a shudder of horror. Thank heaven that was behind her now. She need never again be the biddable possession of any man, much less a cruel control freak. The knowledge of her new-found independence still took her breath away.

Yet a sixth sense kept Callie on edge. Something was wrong. This wasn't pre-party jitters.

'What is it, Angela? What's the matter?'

Her cousin cast a furtive glance to the doorway. 'This visitor.' Her voice was a shaky whisper. 'Papa is arranging for me to marry him.'

'Arranging to marry?'

Callie's lungs seized as horror gripped her. The world spun chaotically and she grabbed the back of a nearby chair.

The years slid away. Once again she was just eighteen, Angela's age. She stood here, waiting alone for him to arrive. The man her uncle had informed her she had to marry.

Unless she wanted to destroy her family.

'Callie?'

Angela's voice pierced the fog of nightmare reminiscence. Callie blinked, clearing her blurry vision and strove for composure.

Another arranged marriage. Another disaster.

Callie groped for Angela's hand, knowing how much her little cousin needed her now. Remembering...

The sound of the men approaching sliced through her garbled thoughts. Her uncle's forthright tone echoed from the foyer but his guest's voice, though pitched low, was more resonant. It pulsed through her, tightening her stomach muscles with an illusion of familiarity.

She thrust aside the absurd idea. Angela's news had knocked her off balance. As had an unexpected afternoon of passion with the sexiest man on the planet.

How she wished she were with him now, rather than in this suffocatingly opulent room, facing another catastrophe of her uncle's devising.

Callie breathed deep. Angela needed her support. She couldn't give in to weakness no matter how shocked she was.

'Let's get through dinner then talk.' She aimed a reassuring smile at her cousin. 'He can't force you into anything. Remember that.'

Angela looked doubtful but there was no time for further conversation. The men were approaching.

Again the timbre of their visitor's voice caught at something inside Callie. Something that had awakened today beneath the sheltering pines and the sensuously heavy touch of a man. It made her pulse trip to a faster, rackety beat.

Ignoring the strange sensation, she stepped forward. She only managed a single pace before jolting to a stop.

Uncle Aristides wore a wide smile as he looked up at the man beside him, then turned to gesture expansively to the room at large.

'Well, my dears, here is our guest. I'd like to introduce a valued business associate, Damon Savakis.'

Time shattered in splintering, razor-edged shards as Callie saw their visitor. A flutter of reaction started high in her throat and her breath faltered. Her heartbeat raced as she took him in. Surreptitiously she snagged a quick, desperate breath, then another.

She stood frozen, staring as shock slammed into her.

Elegant. That should have described him. He wore his dinner jacket as if born to it, with a debonair grace that proclaimed his utter confidence. But the tailored perfection couldn't conceal the man beneath. A man who vibrated energy and authority. A man with the posture and physical perfection of a born athlete.

His face was breathtaking, a sculpted embodiment of male power and sensuality. Except for one thing: his nose sat slightly askew, as if it had been broken. That only emphasised his charisma and an undercurrent of raw masculinity. This was no charming lightweight, but a man to be reckoned with.

His eyes narrowed as he took her in, a glitter of appraisal barely veiled. That searing look did curious things to her insides.

Callie's mouth dried. Dimly she was aware of her uncle drawing Angela forward for an introduction.

Finally, far too late, she stepped forward, her hand outstretched as she dredged up a polite greeting.

'How do you do, Kyrie Savakis? It's a pleasure to meet you.'

His warm hand engulfed hers. She repressed a shiver at the echo of memory that sped through her. Of a man touching her, far more intimately, only this afternoon.

She pulled back but his hold was firm and unbreakable, his look piercing.

Dampness hazed Callie's brow as, for an instant, panic flared. Her stomach churned and she gulped down a hard knot in her throat. Then a lifetime's training kicked in. She ignored the jumble of emotions whirling inside and pinned a meaningless smile to her lips.

Damon Savakis' eyes were dark. Darker than brown. Dark as a moonless night. Dark enough to sweep a woman into a whirlpool of need and longing and hold her there till sanity fled.

Callie knew it because she'd seen them before. Had already experienced the heady invitation of that bold, sensuous gaze.

He spoke at last, his voice brushing across her skin in an intimate tone that made the hairs rise at her neck.

'It's a pleasure to meet you, Callista.' The words were trite, expected, polite. Nothing at all like the searing expression in his fathomless gaze.

Nothing at all like the lazy, sensual approval in his laughing eyes as he'd seduced her a few short hours ago.

CHAPTER TWO

CALLIE'S lungs emptied as his gaze pinioned her.

It *was* him!

There was a roaring sound in her ears, like a jet coming in to land. In the distance her uncle spoke. Yet here, close to *him*, there was nothing but the fire in his eyes. Its impact devastated her, obliterating all thought of what she should do or say. Leaving only a yearning so strong it consumed her.

He was to marry Angela?

Impossible. It was a mistake.

But her uncle didn't make such mistakes.

Callie wanted to smooth her palm along the sharp angle of his jaw to make sure he was real. She wanted to inhale the heady male scent of his burnished skin. She wanted...

No!

Her stomach cramped at the idea of explaining to her uncle how well she already knew his special guest.

This afternoon should have been a moment out of time, a once-in-a-lifetime fantasy. A passing aberration.

Now she was face to face with the man who'd persuaded her to shed every defence she'd used to keep the world, and especially men, at a distance. To keep herself safe.

In a moment of terrifying discovery she realised he had power, real, tangible power over her. She'd let him in, casting aside caution, opening her private, vulnerable self to him. Too late now to slam that door shut again.

This afternoon she'd unwittingly opened a Pandora's box of raw emotion and physical longing. Feelings she'd locked away seven years ago had sprung to life.

And now this hunger, this weakness couldn't be denied.

Hunger for a man who was here to woo her cousin.

What had Callie been to him?

Her stomach somersaulted in distress.

Desperate to break the bond of knowledge and need that pulsed between them, Callie turned, gesturing abruptly to the sofas. Her hand looked steady. Only she knew of the fine tremors running through her body.

'Won't you take a seat?' Her voice was cool, almost without inflection. She prayed that no one else noticed her brittle control over her vocal cords. Tension sank talons into the rigid muscles of her neck and shoulders.

'After you.' He inclined his head and raised his arm behind her back, as if to usher her towards one of the antique French lounges.

Centimetres separated his palm from the silk of her dress, yet she felt his heat, like a phantom caress in the small of her back. Instantly her spine stiffened.

'No, please. Let me get you a drink. What would you like? A cocktail? Wine, sherry? Or something stronger? We have ouzo, brandy…'

He watched her silently, as if he knew nerves made her babble. Gone was the heat in his gaze. Instead his look was speculative.

'Thank you. A whisky.'

Callie moved quickly towards the bar. 'And you, Uncle?'

'Brandy, of course.' There was a snap in his voice, but Callie barely noticed. She was too busy trying to control the trembling in her legs that threatened to buckle her knees.

Disbelief and shock clogged her brain.

She knew the name Damon Savakis. Who didn't? He ran a company that had interests across the globe, in everything from marinas to luxury-yacht production, from exclusive coastal resorts to shipping lines. His wealth matched his uncanny business acumen, his ability to strike at precisely the right moment, turning an ever greater profit. The pundits said he was sharp, ruthless and had the luck of the devil.

More, he was the Manolis company's biggest rival. Surely her uncle had spoken of him as a threat, not a friend?

Why was he staying in their cove on a beautiful but old yacht?

Had he known who she was all this time? She'd been on the family's private estate. But if so surely he'd have mentioned his connection to her uncle.

And his plans to wed Angela.

Unless he'd deliberately withheld the truth. Callie's breath caught.

Had he got a kick out of seducing her, while arranging to marry Angela? Had he laughed at how easy, how gullible she'd been? Did he enjoy watching her flounder for composure?

Bile rose in her throat as bitter memories surged.

Callie had too much experience of powerful men and their diversions. The way they used women. How had she been so stupidly trusting as to forget? Her first real happiness in seven years had been a betrayal.

She fumbled as she reached for the glasses.

'Here. Let me help you,' he murmured from just behind her. A long arm reached out to snag the corkscrew from her hand. 'You prefer wine?'

The words were innocuous, but his breath on her neck sent tingles feathering across her skin. His body behind hers evoked an intimacy that made every hair on her nape rise in anticipation.

Shame washed through her. She couldn't control her reaction.

Curtly she nodded and stepped aside as he uncorked the wine. She was crowded into the corner as he blocked her view of the room, separating her from the others. His heat enveloped her. Callie's nostrils flared as a familiar scent reached her: all male, all too evocative.

'So we meet again, *Callista*.' His whisper was pitched for her ears alone. Yet in that thread of sound she heard the echo of smug satisfaction.

She raised her eyes to meet his then wished she hadn't. They blazed like a dark inferno, scorching her face, her throat, her breasts, in an encompassing survey that told her he remembered this afternoon in vivid detail.

'You're obviously a very versatile woman. What role are you playing tonight?' Disapproval frosted his gaze and his words, making her shiver.

Callie faltered at the unexpected attack. 'What do you mean?'

He shrugged but the intensity of his stare belied the casual gesture. He watched her like a hawk sighting a fieldmouse. 'From wanton to well-bred society girl in an afternoon.' His lips pulled back in what might be a grimace of distaste. 'You look like butter wouldn't melt in your mouth. But just a few hours ago you were seducing a total stranger. Are you always this *adaptable*?'

Callie's vocal cords jammed at his calculated insult. It was true what he said, and yet...after what they'd shared, how could he be so disapproving? Why?

She hadn't been the only one hot and eager down on that beach. How dared he judge her?

'As adaptable as *you*, Kyrie Savakis.' The words nearly choked her.

For an endless moment their eyes meshed. Heat bloomed in her cheeks and she jerked her gaze away, only to find her attention snagging on his hand as he held the wine goblet out to her. He had a workman's hands. Long-fingered but capable, powerful. His grip on the delicate glass should have seemed incongruous. Yet nothing could be further from the truth.

He slid his index finger up the fragile stem then down again. Her mouth dried as she remembered the way he'd touched her nipples with that same finger. The way darts of sensation had rayed out from his touch, making her squirm with delight. The way she'd moaned into his mouth as he'd caressed her and discovered her intimate secrets.

Watching the slow, deliberate movement, feeling the heat of his scrutiny on her flesh made her feel vulnerable. Naked.

Impossible that her body should betray her so. Disgust filled her.

Hurriedly she took the glass from his hand, careful not to brush his fingers. She pushed a tumbler of whisky along the bar towards him.

He was too quick, his hand closing around the glass and her fingers in a grip that made her still.

'What are you doing over there?' her uncle grumbled. 'Callista, you mustn't monopolise our guest.'

'Coming, Uncle,' she called, trying to slide her hand from Damon Savakis' hold.

'What's the matter, Callista? Aren't you glad to see me?' His voice was as seductive as she remembered. As if she'd imagined his disapproval moments ago.

'As a friend of my uncle's you're welcome here,' she said through numb lips, desperately clamping down on the accusations and questions clamouring for release. What did this man want of her? It seemed impossible he was the same warm, exciting lover who'd given her the precious gift of intimacy and tenderness. A wholeness she'd never known.

Damon's eyebrows tilted down in the hint of a frown. His lips thinned a fraction.

'Not a very convincing welcome, *glikia mou*,' he whispered. 'I would have expected something a little *warmer*.'

A ribbon of searing heat curled through her at his endearment in that deep, rich voice. Her weakness horrified her. How could she respond so to a man who had no shame about seducing her while he was here to court Angela? Who chided her for her promiscuity yet played games of innuendo?

Today had stripped her emotionally bare. The experience

had overwhelmed her. Physical pleasure had been a vehicle for much deeper feelings, even for a tentative, unexpected sense of healing.

Her stomach cramped so savagely she could barely stand. What had meant so much to her was a sick amusement to him.

At last she managed to slide her fingers from under his and reached for her uncle's brandy. She looked pointedly over Damon's shoulder, hanging on to control by a thread. She would *not* make a scene.

'If you'll excuse me, I'll take this to my uncle. It's time we joined the others.'

He didn't move. His eyes and his body held her trapped. He blocked her exit. She looked away, at the precise bow-tie on his perfect white shirt.

'Are you planning to visit me again tonight, Callista? To ensure I feel truly welcome?' His voice dropped to a low note that resonated through her very bones. There was no mistaking his blatant sexual invitation. The innuendo and exultation.

Panic welled. And distaste. She felt raw and vulnerable.

He'd deliberately tricked her, luring her into betraying her innermost needs and desires. Desires she'd never known before. Now he wanted to gloat. To turn her one bright, glowing slice of heaven into something sordid.

'Callista?'

She looked up into his shadow-dark eyes, catching the gleam of hunger there and a hint of amusement.

He thought this situation funny?

Instantly her spine straightened. Her chin tilted as indignation and hurt heated her blood. She'd had her fill of the malicious games men played. Of being a pawn, subject to a man's whim.

'You want the truth?' she whispered hoarsely. 'You don't belong here, *Kyrie* Savakis. The last thing I want is to be forced to share a meal with a man like you.'

She stepped forward, calling his bluff.

He had no option but to make way.

Yet the flash of surprised anger in his glittering eyes told her he didn't like it.

Tough! He'd had his little game at her expense. No doubt he'd got a kick out of seducing the woman the gossip mags had dubbed 'untouchable'.

Nausea churned in her stomach and an icy chill crawled through her. She'd believed today was precious. An oasis of warmth and comfort in a cold world.

Fool. Hadn't she learned better than to trust a man?

'That is the way you want to play, Callista?'

There was a warning edge to his tone. She ignored it.

'I don't *play*, Kyrie Savakis.'

She had a swift glimpse of narrowed, calculating eyes, of a chin jutting with masculine displeasure.

He was like the rest, expecting her to bow to his whims. But she was her own mistress now, free and independent.

Nevertheless her heart pounded as she walked past him. The sensation of his eyes on her bare back was like a lick of flame down her spine.

How was she going to survive a whole evening with him?

She had a sinking feeling that instead of her defiance dampening his conceit, he thought she'd thrown down the gauntlet.

He didn't look the type to ignore a challenge.

'No, thank you.' Damon shook his head as the servant proffered wine to top up his glass.

'Come, come, Damon.' His host waved an arm impatiently across the table. 'No need to be abstemious. It's not as if you're driving. Drink up, man.' He nodded to the waiter and watched as his own glass was filled with premium vintage champagne. 'You'll only find the best quality in this house.'

'I don't doubt it,' Damon responded. He looked from the uniformed servants clearing away plates to the ostentatious gold cutlery laid with such meticulous precision on the damask tablecloth. Not many people seeing the luxury in which

Aristides Manolis lived would suspect how parlous was his financial state. How close he was to ruin.

Damon knew. Damon was the man whose money could save Manolis and his family company.

Or destroy it.

He'd worked his adult life for the day he'd have Manolis in his power. The need to acquire and then take apart his precious company piece by piece had driven Damon for years. Revenge for what this family had done to his would be sweet.

A flash of light caught his eye and he turned. Callista's necklace caught the light. A fabulous piece, white gold and several carats of diamonds. Yet it was too obvious for his taste. Too showy. A blatant statement of wealth.

She reminded him of so many other rich, spoiled women he'd known. It was the cost of the gems that mattered to them, not the merit of the design.

Looking at her now, in her exquisite couture gown, her expression bland, he couldn't believe her the same woman who'd seduced him so wantonly. That woman had revealed such vitality and innate sensuality. There'd been something honest about her abandon. Something warmly generous and, he'd almost believed, *special* about her.

He'd responded to her with a hunger that stunned him. He'd spent the hours since anticipating the next day. When, he'd vowed, he would learn more about the woman who intrigued him more than any lover he could recall.

How could he have been so gullible?

'You're admiring my niece's jewellery?' There was gloating satisfaction in his host's voice. He enjoyed flaunting what he had, or pretended to have. Any man who required two staff members to serve a meal for four was trying too hard to impress. 'It's quite something, isn't it?'

Callista looked up then, her face a polite, gorgeous mask. But when her gaze met Damon's he felt again that visceral pull, the drag of spiralling anticipation.

It infuriated him. He should be able to master this raw craving now he knew who and what she was. A pampered member of the Manolis family who'd targeted what she thought was a bit of rough on the side.

Her sensual abandon, her responsiveness had enchanted him on the beach. But from the moment tonight she'd stared at him with blank eyes and chilly hauteur he'd realised today's interlude had been just a jaded socialite's cheap thrill.

If not something more contrived.

He shot an assessing look from his host to Callista.

'The necklace is stunning,' he murmured.

His gaze followed the fall of diamonds on her pendant, the way they dipped into the valley between her ripe breasts, visible in the low-cut gown.

She knew how to show off her assets. The thought annoyed him. Or perhaps it was the cool way she surveyed him with those amazing green eyes that infuriated him. He wasn't used to women, particularly women he'd made love to so thoroughly, being indifferent to him. Or telling him he was unworthy to share their table.

One taste of her had left him craving more. He'd planned to look for his siren lover tomorrow. Now he discovered his fantasy woman was nothing but a spoiled rich girl who was ashamed of what they'd shared.

Ashamed of him.

That idea scored his pride, uncovering old wounds he thought he'd buried a lifetime ago. His slow-burning anger ignited at her dismissal, and at the fact he even cared.

Perversely her cool-as-a-cucumber air ignited his desire. He couldn't resist a challenge. Not while she tried to put him in his place like a dirty secret. As if, despite his wealth and power, a blue-blooded Manolis wouldn't sully her fair skin by letting a man with his working-class roots touch her again.

'Alkis' taste was always excellent, wasn't it, my dear?'

'He certainly knew what he wanted, Uncle.' Her voice was crisp and uninflected, as if she discussed tonight's meal rather than the thousands of euros of gems that dripped down to her breasts. She took her wealth and her life of pampered indolence for granted.

'Alkis?' Damon queried.

'My husband.' Her eyes dropped in an expression that might have been demure if not for the flamboyant glitter at her slender neck, ears and wrist.

Her husband. The syllables thrummed in his ears. Something hard and cold lodged in his belly. Fury sizzled along his veins.

He should have guessed. She was a bored society wife, looking for a little diversion. That was what today's escapade had been.

She'd used him.

Unbidden, memories crowded thick, of the days before he'd made his money. When his only assets had been his determination and his flair for commerce. And his looks. Rich women had clustered round him then, eager for adventure, the thrill of walking on the wild side.

As if he'd swallow his pride to be any woman's plaything.

'Your husband isn't here with you?' Damon reined in brewing anger and self-disgust at having given his libido free rein without checking exactly who she was.

Wide eyes lifted to meet his across the table. They were the colour of the sea in the secluded cove where his yacht was moored. The sea whose lapping waves had muffled the sound of this woman's cries of ecstasy as she found release in his arms.

For a moment he felt again that illusion of oneness they'd experienced as their bodies joined. He'd felt more pleasure with her than he could remember with any woman.

That alone stoked his distrust. And his disgust that he'd fallen for the fantasy she projected.

'My husband died some months ago, Kyrie Savakis.' A chill shuttered the momentary warmth in her eyes.

Too late, Callista! She might act the ice maiden now but he'd already discovered the sensuous fire that blazed inside.

Her passion today hadn't been the by-product of grief for her husband. There'd been no shadowy spectre between them, no yearning for the past. Just untrammelled lust.

A merry widow indeed.

'My condolences,' he said and she inclined her head fractionally. She was so aloof. Not a trace of bereavement or even regret. Damon wondered what sort of female could lose a spouse and not feel anything. Instinct told him, whatever she concealed with that cool expression, it wasn't a broken heart.

'Alkis always chose the best,' Manolis boomed. 'Those diamonds are of the finest quality.'

'Really?' Damon leaned forward as if to get a better look. 'They're quite unusual.' If it was unusual to expend a fortune on something so gaudy. 'I don't think I've ever seen anything to match them.'

'They were made to order. Callista, give our guest a closer look. No need to stand on ceremony, girl.'

'Uncle, I'm sure he doesn't really want to see—'

'On the contrary,' Damon cut across her. 'I'd very much like to see them up close.' If the Manolis clan was vulgar enough to flaunt its apparent wealth, he was happy to take advantage of the fact.

He watched a swift unreadable glance pass between Callista and her silent cousin. Then she rose and walked round the table towards him.

Her exquisite body shimmered seductively and his groin tightened. Lamplight caught thousands of tiny silver beads on her dress. Each step accentuated her lithe lines and sultry curves in a shifting play of light. His muscles tensed with the effort of sitting still and not reaching out to touch. To claim her as, even now, he hungered to do.

When she stood before him he caught a waft of scent that he knew retailed for an exorbitant price. He'd bought some as a parting gift for his last mistress.

He got up, annoyance flaring as he realised he preferred the fresh, natural fragrance of her bare skin this afternoon. The artificial scent masked that.

Yet it served to remind him the woman he'd met earlier, the woman he'd been drawn to, was a fake.

Callista stood, her breasts rising and falling rapidly, making the stones flash and glitter. To his mind she'd look better without them. Just bare golden skin to match the dark-honey hair piled up in a chic style behind her head.

Damon reached for one drop earring. She trembled and the stones scintillated. The fine hairs on her arms stood up, signalling her awareness of him. It couldn't be a chill on a night so warm. Damon's body stirred, attuned to her tension.

He enjoyed the knowledge that she wasn't as calm in his presence as she appeared.

'Remarkable,' he murmured, stepping in so his body almost touched hers, as if to view the heavy pendant. Instead his eyes traced her décolletage. His palms itched as he remembered the bounty of her breasts in his hands.

'They are, aren't they?' Manolis' voice had a self-congratulatory ring. 'Alkis always got his money's worth.'

'I'm sure you're right.' Damon stared into her sea-green gaze, close enough now for him to note again the gold flecks that had dazzled him earlier.

What had her price been?

He'd realised now, remembered the story. A pity he hadn't made the connection earlier today. His enquiries about the Manolis family had revealed only a daughter, no scandalous niece.

This was the woman who at nineteen had been the talk of Athens when she married a rich Greek-American more than old enough to be her father. She'd cashed in her youth and good looks for his wealthy lifestyle and prestigious name, selling herself as a trophy wife.

Damon had been in the Pacific at the time, finalising work on a luxury marina complex. On his return everyone had talked of the match. Now he knew why. Callista was stunning, one of the loveliest women he'd met.

His lips twisted wryly. Like her name, Callista was most beautiful. But that gorgeous body hid a strong mercenary streak. A heartlessness that had enabled her to sell herself for a life of pampered luxury.

Deliberately he turned away, catching the startled gaze of the other woman present. 'But sometimes it's not fabulous jewels that are most alluring,' he said in a low voice. 'Sometimes a more natural style is the most attractive.'

He caught the sound of a hastily stifled gasp beside him. Callista would be used to holding centre stage at the expense of her quiet cousin. She must have read the insult in his words.

'You're right, Damon. Absolutely right.' Manolis boomed in that over-hearty voice as Callista resumed her seat on the other side of the table, her face expressionless. 'Sometimes true beauty is more subtle.'

Subtlety wasn't a trait Damon's host possessed. There was no mistaking his eagerness as he extolled his daughter's virtues, as if she were a thoroughbred in an auction ring. Nor could Damon miss the younger girl's embarrassment as her father's bluff encomiums continued so long.

Damon's eyes narrowed as he sized up the situation.

Did Aristides think he, Damon Savakis, who could take his pick of women, would be interested in a shy little mouse who couldn't even look at him without blushing? Under her father's watchful gaze she stumbled into halting conversation of the blandest sort. Then Manolis began blathering about the importance of family connections, of trust between those who had personal as well as commercial interests in common.

Damon's lips firmed. So that was the way the wind blew. Manolis hoped Damon would fix his interest on his host's daughter.

The man was mad.

Or, perhaps, more desperate than he'd realised. Did he know Damon intended to dismantle his company?

Damon's gaze flicked to Callista. If their passion had meant anything she couldn't be happy about her uncle's matchmaking plans. Yet she looked regal and unruffled, if a trifle stiff. Her message was clear: she'd had her little adventure but now it was over.

Had she acted on her own behalf when she offered herself to him today? A rich woman looking for a tumble with what she thought was a working-class lover? His mouth tightened in distaste. He'd met the sort years ago.

Or had Aristides Manolis planned her convenient visits to the isolated cove?

The notion had been at the back of Damon's mind from the moment he'd found her here, glittering from head to toe like some provocative Christmas gift. The suspicion had made him lash out at her when he arrived, even as he crowded close, unable to keep his distance.

Had Manolis discovered Damon's early arrival to enjoy a low-key, incognito break while recuperating from flu? Had Manolis decided to soften him up before the negotiations began, using his niece as bait? It was the sort of underhand ploy he'd expect from a man like him.

If so, Manolis had miscalculated badly. While she didn't mind slumming it with a stranger for hot sex, obviously her aristocratic pride revolted at having to socialise publicly with a man with working-class roots.

Anger seethed beneath Damon's skin.

Had she bartered her favours to help her uncle, just as she'd bartered her body for a rich husband?

Disgust was a pungent bitterness on Damon's tongue.

Manolis was desperate. Soon Damon would take over the Manolis family company, lock, stock and barrel. The notion warmed the part of his soul that, despite his enormous success, could never quite let go of the past.

There would be satisfaction in crushing Aristides' pretensions and obliterating him commercially.

He was minded to leave and delegate the negotiations to

his lawyers. Only curiosity had prompted him to come. He remembered the awe with which his parents had spoken of the Manolis family that employed his father and grandfather. The company that had finally destroyed them.

Times had changed and the mighty had fallen. Now Damon was the powerful one, the man whose word could make or break this family.

Nothing he'd seen tonight made him feel anything but contempt for his hosts.

And yet…he looked at Callista, felt the slide of her cool gaze glance off his face as she turned to her cousin. Her lips tilted in a half-smile that made his stomach tighten and his breath catch.

Whatever her motives, she'd used him, played him for a fool.

His male pride demanded satisfaction. Damon Savakis was used to calling the shots, not being manipulated.

Yet even now his body hungered for hers with a raw, aching need. This wasn't over. It couldn't be over while he still felt this tide of desire.

He decided in that moment to accept Manolis' offer of hospitality and stay on. Not because the commercial negotiations demanded his presence.

It was business of a much more personal nature he intended to pursue.

CHAPTER THREE

'WHAT do you mean my trust fund is frozen? It can't be.' Only by a supreme effort did Callie keep her voice steady as she stared at her uncle across his over-sized desk. 'I inherit the day I reach twenty-five. That's today.'

He didn't meet her eyes.

That was a bad sign. Usually Aristides Manolis bullied his way out of answering awkward questions. The fact that he didn't attempt it this time set alarm bells ringing. Plus he'd gone to such lengths to avoid a private conversation all week. Finally he'd summoned her to his study after they'd farewelled Damon Savakis.

She shivered despite the sultry air wafting through the open windows. Damon Savakis was someone she didn't want to think about.

Her nerves were raw from an evening of stilted conversation with the man who'd alternately treated her with polite condescension and devoured her with his gaze. The man she'd actually trusted for a few short hours.

'On your birthday, that was the plan,' her uncle said, shifting a silver letter opener. 'But circumstances have changed.'

Callie waited, every instinct alert. But he refused to continue.

'No, Uncle. Not a plan. It's the law.' She took a calming breath. 'My parents set up the trust when I was a baby. Today I inherit the estate they left me.'

She had precious little left of her parents. Memories and a well-worn photo album. When she'd come to live with her Greek relatives, a grief-stricken fourteen-year-old from the other side of the world, her uncle had brusquely informed her that her parents' home would be sold with its contents. It was an unnecessary luxury, he'd declared, storing furniture. Better to plough the proceeds into the fund she'd inherit.

Callie had arrived with only a suitcase and her new lime-green backpack. The one her mum had bought for the sailing holiday they'd planned.

A jagged shaft of pain shot through her, drawing her up straight. Even now memory of that loss had the power to hurt.

'You'll get your inheritance, Callista. It will just take time to organise. I had no idea you'd be in such a rush to access the funds.' His voice had a belligerent, accusing ring. 'What about the money Alkis left you?'

'Alkis left his fortune to his children, as you well know. I'm sure that was covered in your negotiations over my marriage.' A tinge of bitterness crept into her voice. She cleared her throat, determined not to get sidetracked. 'What was left I spent paying his debts. Which is why I want to sort this out. I need the money.'

Callie had plans for her future but she needed her money to achieve them. She'd sell the last of her gaudy jewellery when she left here and put the cash to good use, starting a small retail business. She'd make her own decisions and run her life without interference.

She'd learned her lesson. The only way to be happy was to rely on no one but herself. She knew what she wanted and nothing was going to stop her achieving her goal.

For the first time in years she felt energised and excited, looking forward to the challenges, hard work and satisfaction of building something of her own.

'Perhaps I should just call the family lawyers and—'

'No!' The word was a bellow that made her pulse jump. Her uncle wrenched his tie undone and slumped back in his chair. 'You were always headstrong and difficult. Why can't you wait instead of badgering me about this?'

Years of practice kept Callie's face impassive though her blood boiled. Headstrong! Over the years she'd allowed the men in her life to lead her from one hell into another. If anything she'd been too submissive, too stoic. She'd had enough, starting now.

'Clearly I'm distressing you, Uncle,' she said in her coolest tone. 'Don't disturb yourself. I'll go to Athens tomorrow and sort out the legalities myself.'

There was something akin to hatred in his glare. 'It won't do you any good. There's nothing there.'

Callie felt the blood drain from her face. Her uncle never joked, especially about money.

'Don't look at me like that,' he snarled. 'You'll get it. As soon as this deal with Damon Savakis is finalised.'

'What's he got to do with my inheritance?' The freeze she'd felt earlier clamped tight round her chest.

'The family company...hasn't been doing well for some time. There have been difficulties, unexpected labour and resource costs, a market downturn.'

Strange the downturn affected only the Manolis company when rival ones, like Savakis Enterprises, were booming. Aristides Manolis wouldn't expect his niece to know that. He thought the women in his family empty-headed and incapable of understanding even the rudiments of business.

'And so?' Callie sank into a chair, grateful for its support. Her knees felt like jelly.

'So when the deal with Savakis goes through, this...temporary cash crisis will be rectified.'

'No, Uncle. Even if the deal succeeds, that doesn't explain my trust fund.'

Aristides' fingers tightened on the paper knife with barely repressed violence. His gaze slid away. 'Things were so difficult with the company; I had to find a way to keep it afloat. A temporary measure to tide us over.'

A burning knot of emotion lodged in Callie's throat, choking her, making it difficult to breathe. She squeezed her eyes shut, hearing only her desperately thudding pulse.

How many times would this man betray her?

Why had she naïvely believed that finally, for the first time in her life, things would work out right?

Greed and betrayal. Those were the constant themes in her adult life. You'd think she'd have learned to expect them by now. Yet the shock and hurt, the disbelief, were as overwhelming now as they'd been each time she'd been victim of a man's duplicity.

Wearily she opened her eyes and gazed at the mottled face of her dead father's brother. The one man who, above all, she should have been able to trust.

'You stole my inheritance,' she whispered.

'Callista Manolis! Recall your place! Now that your husband is dead I'm the head of your family.'

'I know who you are.' She thrust aside the panic, the distress, the sheer pain of this ultimate betrayal. 'And *what* you are.' His eyes bulged but he said nothing. 'I thought you'd have more pride than to steal from your own family.'

His fist smashed down on the desk but Callie didn't even blink. 'It wasn't stealing. It was a temporary redistribution of funds. You wouldn't understand—'

'I understand you're a thief,' she said, holding his gaze till he looked away. 'As my trustee you were supposed to behave legally and ethically.'

Callie battled rising fury. She was tempted to report him to the authorities, now, tonight. To see just one of the men who'd used her for their own purposes brought to book.

But the thought of her cousin and her dear aunt stopped her. Justice would hurt them and it wouldn't get her inheritance back.

'The money will be available soon.' His voice was as close to pleading as she'd ever heard it. 'With interest. When this deal goes through.'

'You're expecting Damon Savakis to bail you out of strife?' Hysterical laughter bubbled up inside her. 'His reputation is formidable—as a winner, not for compassion to rivals. He has no interest in helping you.'

'But we won't be rivals.' Aristides leaned forward, his plump hands splayed on the polished wood. 'If my plans go as I expect, Damon Savakis will be more than a business associate. He'll be a member of the family.'

The sound of voices at the poolside stopped Callie in her tracks. Her cousin Angela and Damon Savakis. No other man could unsettle Callie with the low rumble of his laughter. His deep tones made something shiver into life in the pit of her stomach.

Only yesterday, with her face pressed to his broad chest, she'd felt his lazy amusement bubble up and emerge as a deep chocolate caress of sound. Through a haze of sensual satiation it had made her feel vibrantly alive.

Her fingers clenched as desire pulsed again.

She was a fool. He'd used her for cheap amusement in the most calculating way. She'd taken him at face value, believing he, like she, had been blown away by an attraction too strong to be denied.

She suspected with Damon Savakis nothing would ever be simple.

His behaviour last night punctured that foolish daydream. He'd found her amusing. Her confusion and distress had added spice to the evening. How piquant, having his lover and soon-to-be-fiancée together.

She knew his reputation for meticulous attention to detail. Impossible that he hadn't known who she was on the beach. Members of the Manolis family would have been basic research.

But he'd kept his identity a secret, enjoying the joke on her. Seducing the woman dubbed the Snow Queen must have been diverting to an appetite jaded by over-eager women. Watching her squirm last night had been a bonus to a man who revelled in power.

The sort of man she detested.

She straightened her shoulders.

'Good morning, Angela. Kyrie Savakis.' She bestowed a brief smile as she approached the table where she and Angela often shared a meal. No chance now of a private chat. They'd missed their opportunity last night when Uncle Aristides called her to him. Afterwards Callie hadn't found Angela. She hated to think of her alone and distressed.

'Sorry I'm late. I didn't realise we had a guest.'

'Kyrios Savakis is staying with us for a few days,' Angela said quietly, sending a shiver of apprehension down Callie's spine.

A few days! This got worse and worse.

'He arrived for breakfast.' Angela sounded calm and relaxed, a perfect hostess. Only someone who knew her well would realise her discomfort, her fingers busy pleating the linen tablecloth, her body a fraction too poised.

Callie's heart stalled as guilt smote her. She hadn't thought of her poor, shy cousin acting as hostess alone. She'd slept late after a night grappling with what her uncle had conceded about their bleak financial situation. Reliving the horror of discovering Damon's identity and true character.

'Your uncle kindly invited me to sample more of your hospitality,' a deep voice murmured from across the table.

Did she imagine a wry emphasis on the last two words? As if he referred to a service she might personally provide?

He couldn't be so crass. Could he?

Slowly Callie turned to face him, ignoring the escalating thud of her pulse.

He looked disgustingly self-satisfied. Like a man whose appetites had been sated. Callie was horrified at the drift of her thoughts. She forced a smile to her lips, hiding her shudder of reaction as she drank in the sight of him.

Despite her anger, he looked good enough to eat.

If you had a taste for danger.

He wore a white shirt open at the throat, designer jeans and an expression that proclaimed him utterly at home as he leaned back in his seat.

'I was about to show Kyrie Savakis the guest bungalow,' Angela explained.

The guest bungalow? Thank heaven. At least they wouldn't share a house.

'Please, call me Damon. Kyrie Savakis makes me feel like I belong to your father's generation. There's no need for formality.'

But there is, Callie thought, sliding a glance at Angela.

Even after a night coming to grips with her uncle's outrageous plot, Callie couldn't suppress horror at how history repeated itself so appallingly. Her skin crawled. It was a nightmare that he'd use such a scheme a second time.

'Thank you, Damon. Please call me Angela.'

'Angela.' He bestowed a brief smile then turned to spear Callie with his dark, questioning gaze.

'Technically speaking, you *do* belong to another generation.' Callie said before he could speak to her. 'You're in your late thirties, aren't you? Angela is just eighteen.'

Dark brows inched together, then his lips quirked in what looked suspiciously like humour rather than annoyance. 'I'm thirty-four, since you're wondering,' he murmured.

'Really? So—er—young?' Callie arched her brows as if in surprise. She knew when he was born. She'd looked him up on the net last night. He was too old for Angela. As well as the years between them, there was a gulf of experience and expectation that would never be breached. Callie knew it from bitter personal experience.

'Old enough to know my mind, Callie.' The sound of her name on his lips sent a shock wave trembling through her, like the silent aftermath of a sensory explosion. 'May I call you Callie? Or would you prefer Callista?'

She'd prefer neither. Both were far too intimate, especially when he used that smoke and velvet tone guaranteed to seduce a woman out of her senses in thirty seconds flat.

Yesterday just the sound of his voice and the slumberous promise in his eyes had her eager for his touch.

'I...' It was on the tip of her tongue to tell him to use her full name, when she caught Angela's anxious gaze. 'Of course, call me Callie.'

She was only Callista to her uncle, who managed to invest the syllables with disappointment and disapproval.

'Thank you, Callie.' His ebony eyes gleamed with a light she couldn't interpret. His expression sent awareness tingling through her blood. It took a moment for her to realise Angela had turned to talk to one of the staff.

'Would you excuse me?' She rose from her seat. 'There's a phone call I need to take.'

Callie saw the blush on Angela's cheeks and knew Niko must have rung. The son of a local doctor, he'd loved Angela for years. He was building his tourism business, hoping to win Uncle Aristides' approval for their marriage.

Callie knew better than anyone Aristides would never countenance his daughter marrying a local boy, no matter how decent or how much in love they were. Money and status were what mattered to her uncle.

Her gaze shifted to Damon Savakis, lolling in his seat sipping coffee. She felt anxiety shimmy down her spine, knowing what Aristides planned for his daughter.

With those dark good looks and air of leashed power, Damon could model for a pasha of old, accustomed to sumptuous luxury, sensuous pleasures and unquestioning obedience. He'd devour poor Angela in one snap of his strong white teeth then seek amusement elsewhere. As he'd found it yesterday, seducing Callie then playing games of innuendo through the long evening while she squirmed and suffered.

One sacrificial lamb in the family was enough! Callie had performed that function for the Manolis clan years ago. They couldn't demand another.

She refused to watch her uncle ruin his daughter's life with an arranged marriage as he'd ruined hers. Especially when Angela had a chance for happiness with an honest, caring man. That sort of man was as rare, in her experience, as a snowstorm on Santorini.

'Don't hurry, Angela. I'll look after our guest.'

'That sounds promising.'

'Pardon?' Callie turned to find Damon surveying her with a smile that didn't reach his eyes.

'I like the idea of you,' he drawled, 'looking after me. What did you have in mind?'

Heat danced in that calculating expression. His gaze trawled down to her jade top gathered in a knot below the bust, and lower to her bare midriff. Fire blazed over her skin as if he stroked his callused palm over her flesh.

Only yesterday...

Callie shoved back her chair, ignoring the juice she'd poured. 'Showing you the guest bungalow,' she said in a voice that was almost steady.

When he looked at her that way she couldn't prevent the surge of reaction as her body came alive.

She wished she'd worn something other than lightweight trousers and a skimpy top. If she'd known he was here she'd have opted for a full-length tunic dress. But the gleam in his eyes told her it would have done no good. He remembered what she looked like naked.

Just as she remembered him.

He stood, his long, athletic frame unfolding from the chair. She had instant, dazzling recall of how he'd looked yesterday, all burnished skin and honed, hard-packed muscle.

She drew a shuddering breath and looked away, trying to control the riot of hormones clamouring for gratification.

'Ah, Callie, is that all?' One long finger traced the side of her neck and she jumped, jerking out of reach. 'I'd hoped for something a little more...intimate.'

'You—' she sucked in a ragged gasp '—are pushing your luck!'

She lifted her chin, summoning the veneer of composure she'd perfected over the last few years. Ruthlessly she ignored the effervescent sensation of burgeoning desire and strolled to the edge of the terrace, back straight and face composed. It horrified her to discover how difficult it was to don her defensive armour. Only when she had her voice under control did she pause.

'The guest quarters are this way.'

Damon watched her precede him down the lawn. Her hips swayed seductively and his hungry gaze focused on the delicious curve of her *derriere*, shown off perfectly by tight white trousers. Had she worn them to tease? Even in the bright sunlight he saw no panty line to mar the snug fit of cotton against flesh. Did she wear a thong or was she naked beneath the trousers?

Heat roared through him in an infuriating surge. Wasn't it enough she'd kept him awake all night? He'd been angry at how she'd used then rejected him, yet needy for another touch, another taste of her gorgeous body. Even the fact that she'd snubbed him hadn't doused his libido.

'Are you coming?' She stopped and half turned, showing her patrician profile. Even with her hair in a high pony-tail she looked as if she'd stepped from the pages of a glossy magazine, the sort his mother enjoyed. Beautiful, privileged people leading beautiful, privileged lives.

Privileged himself now, with more money and power than a man could ever need, still Damon felt the gulf between himself and such people. It was a gulf he'd consciously created, resisting the artificial lure of 'society'.

He enjoyed his wealth, made the most of what it bought him and those he cared for, but he'd vowed never to succumb to the shallow posturing and brittle selfishness of that world. He'd seen enough as a kid when his mother cleaned villas owned by some of the country's wealthiest families. When as a teenager he'd worked there and learned first-hand about the morals of the upper classes.

Damon was proud of his roots, unashamed that he'd succeeded by hard work and perseverance, not inherited wealth. He'd long ago learned the high-class world of the 'best' people hid an underbelly of greed, selfishness and vice. The last thing on his agenda was attraction to a woman who epitomised that money-hungry shallowness. A woman who'd inherited the Manolis family values.

The fact that he still wanted her annoyed the hell out of him.

'I'm right behind you, Callie.'

He strode to where she waited, mirroring her body with his. He was close enough to feel warmth radiate from her. He leaned forward, head inclined to inhale her scent.

If he'd hoped to discomfit her he was disappointed. With a swish of her pony-tail she led the way in a long-legged stride, riveting his gaze. It took a moment to realise that instead of the rich perfume she'd worn last night, the scent filling his nostrils was the intoxicating fragrance she'd worn yesterday: sunshine and musky, mysterious female.

Lust jagged through him, a blast of white-hot energy.

It confirmed the decision he'd come to last night—there was unfinished business between them. She couldn't brush him aside like some nonentity when she'd had her fill.

'Your colouring is unusual.' He followed her, eyes on the swing of dark-honey hair as it caught the light. He'd picked her for a foreign tourist when he'd first seen her.

She shrugged. 'Maybe I dye my hair.'

'Ah, but Callie, we both know you don't.' The golden-brown triangle of hair he'd uncovered when he stripped away her bikini bottom yesterday had been the genuine thing. 'I've seen the proof, remember? Up close and personal.'

He let satisfaction colour his voice and wasn't surprised when she slammed to a stop ahead of him.

For a moment she stood still, her shoulders curiously

hunched. Then she swung round and met his gaze. Not by the slightest sign did she reveal embarrassment. Her eyes were the colour of cool mountain water, her expression bland. No doubt she was free and easy enough not to feel discomfort discussing personal details with her latest paramour.

What a merry dance she must have led her husband. Had he died trying to satisfy her? Or had he been forced to watch her with younger men who gave her what he couldn't?

'Just as I know your colouring is black as sin,' she murmured. 'So what?' Her brows rose as if she was bored.

'It's uncommon for Greek women to be so fair.' He stepped close enough to see the smatter of gold shards in her irises, like spangles of sunlight amongst the green.

'Half Greek. My mother was Australian.' Her words were clipped, as if he'd delved into something private. He waited for her to continue. 'Besides, some people here in the north have fairer colouring. All the Manolis family are the same.' Her gaze settled on his dark locks as if disapproving.

'Your cousin's hair is brown. There's no comparison.'

He watched her open her mouth as if to shoot off a riposte, then stop herself. She shrugged and turned away. 'Now, if I've satisfied your curiosity—'

'Not yet. Tell me,' he drawled, 'why keep me at arm's length? Surely after yesterday I'm entitled to a little more warmth. Are you one of those women who need the thrill of a secret assignation to fire her blood? Are you turned on by the possibility of being found *in flagrante delicto*?'

Callie stared at the sprawling bungalow a hundred metres down the path and knew it would be a miracle if she made it there with her temper and her composure in place.

Fire her blood, indeed!

Yet she shrank from the suspicion that maybe he was right. Maybe the thrill of desire that had swept her doubts and defences away yesterday was a result of their anonymity and the unspoken daring of their actions.

She shut her eyes, remembering the delicious excitement as he'd walked towards her through the dappled shade, his eyes never leaving hers so she felt the tug of his powerful personality like a living force. Without pause or hesitation he'd pulled her into his arms as if she belonged there. She'd welcomed each caress with a fervour that frightened her now.

Nothing had ever seemed so right, so perfect.

Callie snapped open her eyes. She'd given him too much already. She wouldn't let him toy with her while he played games of one-upmanship with her uncle. While he decided whether to take her cousin in a cold-blooded business deal.

She was done with being a pawn in any man's machinations.

'You're not *entitled* to anything from me.'

She fixed him with the cool look she'd perfected long ago to hide desperately churning emotions. Alkis had had no patience with emotion in his wife. Retreat behind her façade of indifference had been a hard-won but necessary survival skill.

'I disagree. After yesterday your attitude is downright unfriendly.'

Damon paced closer. She had to lift her head to hold his gaze. His heat curled round her like an invitation. The scent of soap, sea and healthy male enticed her till it was an effort not to reach out needy fingers for one last caress.

Callie slid her hands into her trouser pockets lest she be tempted to do something insane like touch him.

'Yesterday is over.'

'But what we had needn't be.' His low, seductive voice pierced her brittle façade. He made her yearn again for the delicious torment of his touch.

That terrified her.

'It's over,' she repeated, wishing she believed it.

'And if I'm not ready to end it?' His look was arrogant.

'There was nothing to end.' The words tumbled out. She had to concentrate on slowing down, maintaining her calm. 'We had sex. That's all.'

'Just sex.' His brows winged up and she thought she saw fury blaze in his eyes. Then the moment was gone and his face was unreadable. 'Is that what you specialise in, Callie? Hot sex with strangers you forget the next day?'

Her skin crawled with embarrassment and rage. Yet she knew better than to show it. She let her gaze drop to his shoulders, his wide chest, the powerful length of his arms and legs, then slowly up as if she were used to inspecting the finer points of a sexy male body.

'I could say the same for you,' she said, silently cursing the dry mouth that made the words come out too husky. 'You got what you wanted yesterday. End of story.'

'You're wrong, my fine lady. It's not the end at all.'

A tremor ran through her body, drawing each muscle tight with…anticipation? Excitement?

No! She refused to play his games of seduction and temptation. Yesterday had been a terrible error of judgement. She'd broken every precept, her own moral code, for a few hours' passion. It had been momentary insanity.

She should have guessed nothing was as pure and simple as it had seemed at the time.

'Believe me, Kyrie Savakis, it's over. Why not move on?' Callie had no doubt by nightfall he'd find another woman eager to become a notch on his bedpost. As she had been yesterday. Her chest constricted painfully.

'Because I'm a man who gets what he wants, *glikia mou*. You've whetted my appetite and I want more.'

His lips curved in a hungry smile that sent fear trickling down her spine.

'I want you, Callie. And I intend to have you.'

CHAPTER FOUR

WHAT the hell had got into him? Even as the words emerged from his mouth, Damon questioned his sanity.

She wasn't the sort of woman he wanted in his life.

Nothing he'd learned about her was positive.

Except for the ecstatic, uninhibited way she responded to sex. In that department she packed enough punch to flatten even his formidable self-control.

The unvarnished truth was once with Callie Manolis wasn't enough. Despite his scruples and his anger he wanted her. Still. More. Again.

He cursed his weakness but couldn't pull back. His need was primal, stronger than reason.

Her eyes widened. Her mouth sagged and he fantasised about plundering it with an urgent kiss that would lead to other, more satisfying activities.

'Your threats don't frighten me.' Yet her voice was husky. She *was* frightened.

Or turned on. Damon's body tensed on the thought.

'No threat. A promise.'

'You have no hold over me.' She lifted her head and bestowed a blazing look, like an Amazon queen, defiant and proud. 'I run my own life. *No* man tells me what to do.'

She gestured to the bungalow at the end of the path. 'I'm sure you can find your own way, Kyrie Savakis.' Then she turned and left him. She strolled easily as if she'd done no more than dismiss a servant.

No one dismissed Damon Savakis.

Yet he silently applauded her nerve. Not many people stood up to Damon.

She fascinated him. He wanted to smash past her poise and warm her body with his till the heat consumed them both.

He tucked his hands into the pockets of his jeans rather than haul her into his arms and force her submission with a direct, passionate assault.

That would be too easy, too crude. He wanted the satisfaction of her coming to him, begging for his attention.

In twenty-four hours Callista had become more than a challenge. She was fast becoming an obsession. Despite her disdain. Despite who she was. Or perhaps because of it.

Old anger stirred. His grandfather and his father had slaved for the Manolis family, wrecking their health for little pay. His grandfather had worked himself into an early grave. When Damon's father died in an industrial accident in the Manolis shipyards his mother had received condolences, a company representative at the funeral and none of the compensation she was entitled to. Lawyers had exploited a loophole to absolve the company of responsibility. As if it wasn't a matter of conscience and honour. As if his father's death had been another entry in a ledger.

Damon had directed his anger into his quest for success, ensuring his family was never again as vulnerable as when he was fifteen, the eldest of five fatherless children.

Was it any wonder he enjoyed watching Aristides Manolis scamper to please him? Or revelled in the idea of Callista Manolis, so dismissive, bending to his will?

Her damnable coolness set the seal on her fate.

Damon would make her confess her desire. He'd take her again, just long enough to have his fill. Then he'd dump her, leaving her craving more. Craving what she couldn't have.

* * *

Callie walked up the hill, resisting the instinct to run. The knowledge that he watched her gave her courage not to flee. That and the fact that her knees trembled so hard it was a supreme effort to move at all.

She felt his hot, possessive gaze like a touch. That proprietorial sweep of her body with eyes so black she fell into oblivion whenever they held hers. Despite her fury her traitorous body was alive with fizzing awareness.

She'd given herself blithely, not realising the danger.

Now she couldn't escape until she sorted out her inheritance. Without that she couldn't realise her dream of establishing a small business and supporting herself.

That dream had kept her going through the cruel years of marriage. It had given her hope. It was too precious to give up. Yet all she could do now was pray her uncle's deal went through and, miraculously, Damon rejected his matchmaking.

She stumbled to a stop as realisation slammed into her. Only Damon's money could save her plans for the future.

Thank God he had no idea. He was unscrupulous enough to use her vulnerability against her.

The sound of weeping interrupted her thoughts. Following it, she came to a secluded grove. There, to her dismay, she found Angela huddled on a bench, shoulders hunched.

Callie froze, memories swamping her.

Déjà vu. Seven years ago she'd come here to sob out her broken heart when the love of her life betrayed her. She'd thought nothing could eclipse her pain and disillusionment.

How naïve she'd been. That had just been the beginning.

'Angela! What is it, sweetie?' She hurried forward and wrapped an arm round her cousin's unsteady shoulders.

'It's Papa,' she sniffed. 'He knew I'd been talking to Niko. He was furious.' She slumped and Callie drew her close.

'He's forbidden you to see Niko?'

Angela nodded.

'Go on.' Callie's heart was leaden. She'd hoped it wouldn't

come to this. Her uncle had let slip last night that Damon hadn't yet agreed to the marriage.

'He won't listen, doesn't care that Niko and I love each other.' Angela wailed. 'He says I have to save the family and the company.'

Callie's arm tightened.

'I tried to reason with him.' Angela's voice was ragged and Callie's chest squeezed, knowing what it had cost her cousin to stand up to her bullying father. 'I said Damon wouldn't be interested in me. I'm not glamorous like you. That only made him angrier. He said Damon wanted children with someone obedient and docile. Someone from a good family to connect him with the right sort of people.'

Callie cringed at her uncle's prejudiced views. As if Damon needed marriage to secure his place in society! His authority and massive wealth gave him entrée wherever he cared to go. Her uncle was a troglodyte.

But in one thing he was right: men still bartered wealth to possess women. Her uncle had cashed in on Alkis' obsession with Callie to shore up the family coffers last time he'd mismanaged the company. Callie had been naïve enough to fall in with his wishes, for the good of the family. She'd thought her life over at eighteen and hadn't realised the yoke she'd put around her neck, marrying a man as cruel and controlling, and as insecure as Alkis.

'Papa said a man took a wife to bear children and make life comfortable. That Damon would look elsewhere for…for…'

'Shh, Angela. It's all right.' Bitter fury surged in Callie's veins at her uncle's callousness, treating them like pawns. At the ruthless men who joined his devious games.

'But it's not. If I don't obey we'll lose everything. The house. Everything. And Mama is so sick, more than Papa realises. If she needs treatment…'

Angela sat up, breaking Callie's embrace. Her face was pale and set, despite the tears tracking down her cheeks.

With a last hug Callie let her arm drop, watching Angela's

drawn face with foreboding. Despite her quivering mouth there
was resolution in the tight angle of her jaw.

'You're not alone, Angela. Remember that. I'll help.'

'But what can you do? What can either of us do?'

Callie stood and reached out a hand. Angela let Callie pull
her up. 'Don't give up yet. We'll find something.'

Whatever it took she'd find a way to save her cousin.

She couldn't let Angela endure what she, Callie, had. She'd
walk over hot coals to prevent it.

Callie's lips thinned in a grimace of determination.

She'd get down on her knees and beg Damon Savakis, if
that was what it took.

'Thank you, Callie.' Damon accepted the cold drink, deliberately encircling her slim fingers.

She jumped and sticky juice cascaded over their hands.

Her nerves were frayed, he saw with satisfaction. Her touch-
me-not composure crumbled after days playing hostess to him.
The business could have been concluded in a few hours but
Damon had let Manolis drag out discussions, since it meant
having Callie at his beck and call.

At first he'd thought she'd run. He'd been ready for a chase.
Instead the hunt had become a slow siege, a war of attrition.
With each day the flicker of hunger in his belly grew to a blaze
as he sensed her defences weaken.

She tugged her hand. Damon didn't release her but got up
from the poolside chair, fingers still wrapped around hers.

'Sorry,' she murmured, her gaze skating from his then back
again. 'I've spilled it. I'll go and get a cloth.'

'No need.'

'But I—'

'Let me.'

He lifted their linked hands. Gold sparked in her sea-green
eyes and beneath the high-necked silk top her breasts rose and
fell rapidly. As rapidly as his shortened breathing.

He shifted his hold and bent his head, licking the juice

from her thumb, her forefinger, the sensitive V of flesh between them. A judder ran through her. Only his iron-hard grasp
stopped her dropping the glass.

Her taste was sweet and salt and feminine musk. The scent
of her skin like summer. Instantly his hunger escalated to a
desperate craving. Too late he realised his mistake. The taste
of her sent him spinning out of control. He was rigid with the
force of swelling desire.

'Don't. Please.' Her voice was low but he couldn't miss the
quiver of unsteadiness.

A bolt of something like guilt or even pity cleaved through
him, making him frown. What had happened to the Callista
he knew—all ice and fire? Her self-possession slipped and he
glimpsed a different woman behind the façade.

That was what he wanted, wasn't it? For her to surrender
and admit she wanted him?

Yet looking at her averted profile, reading the fine lines of
strain around her mouth and the smudge of tiredness beneath
her eyes, he knew a moment's doubt.

'Callie,' he murmured, drawing her closer.

'Callie, can you help? I—' Angela's voice came from the
terrace and Damon turned as the younger girl approached.
Her eyes were huge as she took in the pair of them. Belatedly
Damon released his hold. Instantly Callie shifted away. 'I'm
sorry; I just wanted to check something.'

'Hi, Angela. No need to apologise.' Damon smiled. He liked
the girl despite her puffed-up father. She reminded him of his
youngest sister, timid with strangers but delightful.

Callie hurried to Angela, drawing her away. She shepherded
the younger girl, her arm raised as if to protect.

Damon frowned. He'd seen that gesture before. It had taken
this long for him to notice, for whenever Callie was near he
didn't think clearly.

Now he watched and wondered, his brain clicking into gear.
He recollected how regularly Callie appeared when he and
Angela were alone. How she often sat between them.

Why?

The women conferred about a projected dinner party. As if aware of his regard, Callie raised her head and something sparked in her eyes. She excused them and ushered Angela ahead of her into the house.

Could it be that, despite her hoity-toity attitude, Callie was jealous of the attention he gave her cousin?

He turned and paced the length of the pool.

Or had he been right the first time? Was she trying to protect her cousin? The idea nonplussed him.

He'd never be a threat to a sweet girl like Angela. The girl was probably a virgin and far too young. He didn't seduce innocents. Life was less complicated with lovers who understood long term relationships weren't on his agenda.

When the time came to think of marriage he...

Damon stilled.

Was that it? Aristides Manolis' plan to interest Damon in marriage to his daughter? The idea was nonsense. As if he needed help choosing a wife! As if Angela would suit him!

Then he remembered the look on Callie's face as she urged her cousin inside. Could she really believe he was interested in marrying Angela?

Suddenly so much made sense.

A smile of satisfaction spread across Damon's face.

He had her.

He knew the chink in Callie's armour. All he had to do was apply a little pressure.

'Just who I wanted to see.' Damon's voice was low and intimate. The hairs on Callie's neck rose in instant awareness. 'We need to talk.'

It didn't matter that he held her in contempt. Or that he threatened the fragile peace of mind she'd built up since Alkis' death. A force stronger than reason or pride held her in thrall to Damon Savakis.

Who'd have thought desire could be so strong? In her inexperience it had seemed far more—as if in the seclusion of the pine-shaded beach, she'd connected with the only man in the world who was...right.

Her lips thinned. She'd always been too naïve. She should have stopped believing in fantasy long ago.

Slowly she turned. After a morning in her aunt's sick room, Callie had sought the secluded platform at the end of the garden. She'd hoped its view over the village and the sea beyond would help her find the peace she'd lost.

He wore a crisp white shirt and tailored dark trousers, a jacket slung over one solid shoulder. He looked serious, a man to be reckoned with.

He'd been with her uncle for hours. What had they decided?

'I'm leaving soon,' he said, stepping close.

Callie's hands tightened on the balustrade. Relief, not dismay. She told herself she *wanted* him to leave.

'I hope you've enjoyed your stay.' She turned, unable to hold his stare. Instead she gazed at the distant harbour.

'Your family's hospitality has been most...generous.' His odd inflection sent unease skimming down her backbone.

A vessel in the harbour, a tiny blue-hulled boat, chugged towards the open sea. Callie wished she could be on it, sailing safely away from Damon. Her lips twisted. Just the idea of going on board a small boat made her stomach cramp with fear. She couldn't even fantasise about her escape!

'So generous that I'm considering strengthening my connection with your family.'

She should be relieved. If the deal was favourable she might get her inheritance. Yet, turning to see his satisfied expression, she had an awful suspicion it wasn't so simple.

'With a merger?' She held her breath.

He draped his jacket over the railing then leaned, arms splayed. He looked like a man who commanded all he surveyed.

Disquiet thrummed through her. Her uncle had invited a powerful predator into their midst and foolishly believed he could keep the upper hand. Instinct told her Aristides Manolis had badly underestimated Damon.

'Not necessarily.' Was that a hint of amusement? 'I'm considering something more personal.'

Callie's fingers clenched round the rail in spasm.

'Your cousin is a lovely young woman.' There was a purr of satisfaction in his voice that made Callie's hackles rise.

He wasn't serious! He didn't need marriage to a Manolis to cement his place in society. The idea was farcical.

'I don't see the connection,' she said through clenched teeth.

'Don't you? Odd, I thought you quite astute.'

She cast him a surprised glance then looked away.

'Angela will make someone a fine wife,' he mused. 'She has the qualities a man looks for in a permanent partner.'

'What? Timid, eager to please and biddable?' She couldn't keep the sarcasm from her voice. She'd learned what men wanted. Someone to shore up their egos and obey their whims. They didn't look beyond the surface to the woman beneath. Much less recognise her needs.

'Trust a beautiful woman to be so scathing of another.'

'That's not what I meant! I—'

'I'm surprised you don't know your cousin better. I was going to say Angela is intelligent, amiable and generous. Pretty too in her quiet way.'

'She's too young for you,' she blurted out. 'Far too young.' Defiantly she confronted him. The impact of his gaze, so intense, so penetrating, dragged the air from her lungs.

One eyebrow, dark as night, rose speculatively.

'You can't be serious,' she hissed.

'Why not? A man reaches the stage when he wants a woman to come home to.'

'I'm sure you have no problems finding women eager to wait up for you.'

His lazy smile set her teeth on edge. 'You're right. But I'm not talking about casual sex. I'm talking about the mother of my children. A man wants to pass on his name, his genes, his fortune to the next generation.'

Callie had become used to such attitudes since moving to Greece in her teens. Yet the cold-bloodedness of taking a wife simply because it was time to settle down irked her.

'You want a brood mare.'

'More than that.' His expression was amused. 'I require someone to be my hostess too.'

'Why tell me?' she asked flatly.

'You're an intelligent woman. You know your cousin. Your opinion interests me.'

She regarded him through narrowed eyes. There was a catch somewhere. 'It wouldn't work. Angela doesn't want to marry you. She's in love with someone else.'

No male with any pride would stomach the idea of his woman pining for another. Hadn't Alkis' obsessive jealousy arisen from the false belief Callie would seek the passion he couldn't provide in another man's arms? He'd made their lives a misery and their marriage a cruel prison because of it.

Damon merely smiled, like a hungry wolf sizing up its next meal.

'She's eighteen. Of course she fancies herself in love. She'll get over it. Any husband worth the name would see to that.' He straightened, shifting his weight. Callie was struck anew by the sheer masculine charisma of his tall frame. If any man could turn the head of a susceptible teenager it was him.

'You don't understand.' Callie turned and paced, unable to stay still. 'They're really in love. This is genuine.'

'At her age? It's puppy love.'

Callie opened her mouth to argue then snapped it shut. At eighteen she'd been head over heels in love with Petro, a clever, older law student. She'd believed it a grand passion, a once-in-a-lifetime thing.

Callie had been an ugly duckling who'd never felt at home in Greece, or with her new family, and still grieved the loss of her beloved parents. She'd spent four years struggling to fit in where everything, from the language to the customs, was foreign. She'd barely scraped a place at university and had been pathetically grateful when a dashing older student found her attractive.

How easy to seduce her, a gawky eighteen-year-old virgin. Callie had dreamed of happily-ever-after in his lean embrace. Until the day Uncle Aristides descended like Zeus thundering down from Mount Olympus. He was enraged at paying so much money to dispose of a fortune hunter.

Petro had left with never a second glance. Once he had funds at his disposal he'd gone back to his girlfriend.

So much for his protestations of undying love.

Callie had been heartbroken and distraught. Easy prey for her uncle's scheme with his crony, Alkis.

'Callie?'

Damon's baritone dragged her back to the present. She blinked and found she'd wrapped her arms round her torso. Slowly she unwound them and stood straight, looking at a point near his collarbone.

'Angela deserves the chance to marry the man she loves.'

'Don't tell me you believe in romantic love?'

She shrugged, trying to don an air of insouciance. She felt too brittle. As if her façade of control might splinter.

'For some. For Angela.' Not for herself. She'd given up that fantasy long ago.

He dismissed her argument with a single slashing gesture. 'I don't see a problem. Especially with your uncle onside. Between us we can overcome any doubts she has.'

All warmth leached from Callie's body. She knew her uncle's tactics too well. The mixture of blustering threat and heartfelt appeals for the good of the family.

At Angela's age Callie had succumbed and agreed to marry the polite older man who'd payed court so graciously. Too late she'd learned her husband's old-world charm hid a cruel and unstable disposition.

The knowledge filled her with desperate resolve.

'No! You can't. You mustn't.' The words spilled out and she took an involuntary step towards Damon, one hand outstretched in her urgency.

'Mustn't, Callie? You're not in a position to dictate to me.' Damon towered over her, eyes glinting with challenge.

Her hand dropped as fear swamped her. How could she win against this man? What weapons did she have to thwart him?

'Once you're married you're tied permanently.' She'd bet Damon would see a failed marriage as a personal failure. 'Are you ready to settle down and devote yourself to one woman?'

'Why?' Heat flickered in his eyes. His stare was so intense it grazed her cheeks. 'Have you changed your mind about our affair?' He closed the space between them, forcing her to retreat till the balustrade dug into her back.

'No! I just—'

'You just decided you didn't like your little cousin doing well for herself.' Damon's lip curled derisively and Callie's heart dived. She'd never overcome his bias against her. 'You don't like being overlooked. I bet Angela has lived in your shadow for years.'

'That's not true!' Callie had never wanted centre stage. Only Alkis' determination to show her off had propelled her into a social sphere where she'd learned, painfully, to hold her own, despite the barbs and whispered gossip. She looked at Angela and saw herself at eighteen: quiet and far too vulnerable. 'Angela's not a rival, she's—'

A disparaging flick of his hand silenced her. 'I'm not interested.' He paused, eyes pinioning hers. 'Although…'

'Although?' Her hands wrapped around the railing as she straightened. Was he having second thoughts? Hope blossomed.

'One thing might make me reconsider,' he said slowly, one hand rubbing his jaw.

'Yes?' She took a half-step forward before slamming to a halt, suddenly far too close to his big body. His heat shimmered through her, his scent reminding her of intimacies she tried hard to forget.

Damon reached out and cupped her chin with his palm. Her body responded with a thrill of excitement that drew every nerve to attention. Slowly, oh, so slowly, his thumb slid across to her mouth, swiping deliberately across her bottom lip and tugging her lips apart.

She fought to keep her eyes open against the surge of physical longing his touch evoked. Callie's fingers clenched into fists at her sides, the breath catching in her chest till she felt light-headed.

One caress, one touch, did that!

'Yes.' His sibilant stretched out in a hiss of satisfaction as he lowered his head.

She should move. Pull away. Run! But her feet were glued to the spot, her will to resist eclipsed by a flood of remembered pleasure.

'Come to me tonight, Callie. Give me one night and I'll say no to marrying Angela.' The sensuous burr of his voice enthralled her. She had trouble focusing on his words.

His eyes burned dark fire as she stared up into his bold face. This close she saw the way his fine-grained skin began to darken along that chiselled jaw. Not by so much as a blink did he betray emotion. There was just that all-consuming sensuality, drawing her closer.

Stunned, she felt her will soften, her body sway towards him, drawn by the force of a desire she couldn't conquer.

Then her brain clicked into gear. His words percolated through her hazy thoughts. She jerked her chin from his hold, stepping back carefully as if expecting him to lunge for her.

'And if I don't?'

His smile disappeared. His eyes narrowed as anger sparked. 'What do you think?'

'I think you're some piece of work, Damon Savakis.' Callie wrapped her arms round herself, as if to stop the sudden pain that engulfed her. For a moment she'd hoped he felt a little of the magic she'd imagined between them. The reality of his outrageous proposition was too cruel. 'This is a sick game you're playing.'

'No game, Callie. A simple deal.'

'You think you can *buy* me?'

He shook his head. 'Don't play innocent. It doesn't suit you.' He raked her with a searing stare that burned her flesh. 'You've been bought before, remember? When you married your late unlamented husband.'

The horrible truth was like a blow to the solar plexus, winding her and cramping her stomach.

That was different, she wanted to scream. I didn't care about anything then because I thought my life was over. I was hurt and vulnerable and I believed I was saving my family. If only I'd known the mistake I was making.

'But you're asking me to…give myself for your pleasure.'

Damon folded his arms. The movement accentuated the muscles in his arms and chest, and his air of lazy confidence.

'No need to be melodramatic, Callie. I'm not asking you to do anything you haven't done, *and enjoyed*, before.' His mouth pulled wide in a smile of satisfaction that sent the blood tingling through her body.

'That's not the point!' Callie was so furious, so appalled she felt like landing a punch that would bend his arrogant nose completely out of shape.

Her anger was heightened by the knowledge that he was right. She'd enjoyed every moment of their intimacy.

'Then what is? You don't want me to marry Angela. Very well, I'm willing to compromise. I'll take you instead, on a strictly short-term basis. One night. That's all I want.'

He'd never consider *her* as a marriage candidate. He'd want someone pure, innocent and gullible for that role.

Callie's mouth quirked in a humourless smile. That was one thing she'd been saved: a marriage proposal from another arrogant lord-of-all-he-surveyed tycoon.

'What's so amusing?'

'Just relief you're not offering anything permanent.'

His eyes widened, then he jerked his head up in denial. 'Don't hold your breath. A single night will be sufficient.'

'Thank heaven for small mercies,' she muttered. Her pride smarted at his dismissal. But despite her anger heat flared under her skin as his gaze trawled her, slow and assessing. As if remembering how she looked naked.

Was this how slaves felt in the ancient markets, scrutinised by buyers? His glittering appraisal left Callie exposed and vulnerable. Yet a tiny, renegade part of her thrilled, knowing he desired her.

'You're bluffing.' She straightened her shoulders.

'I don't waste my time with bluff.' He paused as if weighing her mood. 'Tonight's my last night here. That's your deadline. Come to me tonight, stay as my lover and the deal will go through without a marriage contract. I'll even allow a fair settlement on the Manolis family.'

He watched her with glittering eyes. 'Tonight,' he repeated. 'I'll be waiting.'

'You'll wait a long time.'

His sensuous lips curved in a smile that did nothing to allay her fears. 'In that case I'll look forward to seeing you dance at my wedding.'

CHAPTER FIVE

DAMON strode across the living room of the opulent guest bungalow, swung round and paced back the way he'd come.

Eleven o'clock.

She wasn't coming.

Hell! He'd been so sure. Certain that at last he'd find respite from the voracious hunger that gnawed his vitals, distracted him from work and kept him from sleep. He speared his fingers through his hair, frustration rising.

He wasn't used to losing. Couldn't remember the last time he hadn't got his way in an important negotiation. And this, for reasons he couldn't fathom, was important.

Callista Manolis got to him as no woman ever had.

She should leap at the chance to share his bed, hoping for the expensive trinkets a man as rich as he could buy her.

But that wasn't her game. She'd sold herself in marriage once. No doubt she was angling for another cushy, long-term position. She set a high price on her favours.

Except when she pursued a little casual distraction with someone she thought unimportant, someone she could use briefly then discard. As she'd used him at the beach. She'd been warm and wanton in her pursuit of pleasure. So uninhibited he'd plunged headlong into a passion that far surpassed any of his recent liaisons.

He slammed to a stop, frustration rising in a tide that tightened every muscle. At dinner tonight she'd worn a dress designed to drive men to the edge of sanity, hinting at barely concealed feminine treasures. He'd taken it as a sign of her capitulation.

Instead the vixen had been toying with him.

He lunged for the sliding glass door and hauled it open, needing fresh air. He strode out to the flagstoned terrace then catapulted to a stop.

She was here.

His breath stopped as relief swamped him. It came in a rush so overwhelming he clutched at the door. Dimly he registered amazement at the intensity of his reaction.

His heart accelerated to a restless, arrhythmic beat as he watched her pick her way down the path from the main house, holding her long skirts up around her ankles.

Fire glittered on her breasts and round her wrist. She'd worn the diamonds again. But it wasn't jewellery that fixed his attention. Each time she passed a glowing uplight on the path it turned the fabric of her dress translucent, hinting at her seductive form.

The gown was long, white, gossamer-fine gathers of fabric designed to look like an ancient Greek dress. Fine gold cords crossed at her waist and below her breasts, defining luscious curves and a slim figure. The neckline plunged so deep she couldn't wear a bra. The silken swish of fabric as she moved was designed, he hoped, to indicate the absence of underwear.

Damon's hands itched to reach for her. He remained where he was.

Let her come to him.

'You decided to accept my offer.' He kept his voice firm, devoid of the raw satisfaction that would betray his pleasure. He would show no vulnerability to this woman.

'How could I resist such an alluring proposition?' The words came low and husky in the darkness, drawing the tension in his belly tighter. Yet even in the dim light there was no mistaking the jeering twist of her lips.

She still feigned distaste. Did she never give up?

She stepped onto the terrace and stood a few metres away, hands concealed in the folds of her dress, chin up, expression glacial. Yet that mask of disdain couldn't conceal everything. Her breasts rose and fell quickly, making the diamonds at her cleavage shimmer.

She wasn't the ice maiden she pretended. Soon she'd thaw for him.

'So what is this?' He waved a disparaging hand at her long dress. 'Your virgin-sacrifice outfit?'

Her lips curled in a tight smile that didn't reach her eyes. 'Hardly. You made it clear it wasn't an innocent you wanted. I thought that's why I appealed—because I've got such *vast* experience with men.'

Callie held her breath, amazed at her temerity in baiting him. She didn't know whether to be horrified or glad she still had strength to trade insults with Damon Savakis. Part of her cringed at what she was doing. The impulse to flee kept her poised for flight.

The idea of agreeing to this cold-blooded arrangement made her stomach churn and her mind revolt. She was so inexperienced she could count on the fingers of one hand the number of times she'd been with a man.

Her as a billionaire's plaything for the night!

Yet she had no choice. She couldn't, wouldn't turn her back on her cousin. No girl deserved to have her life blighted as Callie's had been in a contract marriage. Not where all power rested with an older, powerful husband who saw his wife as a chattel, not a real person with feelings.

That thought steadied her nerves.

'You look stunning,' he murmured. 'You know how to dress to please a man.'

Bitterness twisted in Callie's belly. Alkis had chosen this, as he had all her evening dresses. He'd selected expensive outfits that showed off his wealth and too much of her flesh. Though impotent, her husband had enjoyed making her flaunt herself, despite her protests, or perhaps because of them. He got a perverted kick out of parading her half-naked before other men. As if their thwarted desire compensated for his own inability to consummate the marriage.

He'd revelled in the sight of their tongues hanging out as they undressed her with their eyes. But it hadn't stopped him lashing out at her in private for supposed infidelities.

Oh, she knew all about dressing to please a man. That was why she hated this dress. It made her feel tainted.

'I thought you'd appreciate the dress.' He was like the others, interested only in her body.

'Tell me,' he purred in a voice that rubbed like velvet over her bare flesh, 'are you wearing anything under that?'

Callie's forced smile froze on her lips as a shiver of trepidation swept through her.

Fear threatened to puncture her carefully constructed mask of indifference. For this wasn't like before, when they'd come together in a joyous rush of mutual desire. This was something beyond her ken. There was an edge of danger to this situation. He looked so...predatory, as if he wanted to gobble her up with one snap of his jaws. There was nothing warm or gentle about the hunger in his face.

A *frisson* of stark panic sped down Callie's backbone.

'Would you prefer it if there wasn't?' Surreptitiously one slim heel slid back on the flagstones, till she realised what she was doing and forced herself to stop.

She'd made up her mind to do this. If she didn't please Damon it would be disastrous. This way her family would retain their home and Angela would be free to marry Niko.

Only Callie would be stripped of her dignity, and her privacy. Her mind shied frantically from the thought.

Yet after all she'd endured, she'd survive this. One night. *One long night.* Then she'd be free.

'I like the idea of you coming to me naked beneath the glitter and the haute couture.' He shrugged. 'But it doesn't matter. I'm sure you'll find a way to satisfy me.'

Callie's throat closed on a spasm of horror. How long could she keep up the pretence of indifference? Already she was torn between the desire to curl up and hide and the need to have him show again the tenderness that had obliterated all her defences.

No! She couldn't think like that.

Tenderness wasn't on Damon's agenda. He looked alert, aware, hungry. His stance was a hunter's, ready to attack.

'Aren't you going to invite me in?' He'd been silent so long her nerves stretched thin.

'Of course.' He stood aside and gestured for her to precede him into the lamp-lit sitting room. 'Welcome.'

Said the spider to the fly. Callie shivered at the carnivorous edge to his smile. Her steps were reluctant but she forced herself forward.

If she didn't do this she'd regret it for the rest of her days. She *would* rescue Angela. As she'd wished so often someone had stepped in years ago to save her from making the worst mistake of her life.

That knowledge gave her the strength to slip past him, chin up, eyes straight ahead. She faltered as she caught his scent, warm and intoxicating, and felt a whisper of desire shiver into life. But anxiety extinguished it as she stepped into the shadowed room.

She felt movement behind her and shuffled a couple more paces forward.

The sound of the door sliding closed made her scalp prickle. To her overwrought imagination it was as loud as the thud of a cell door. She licked dry lips then wished she hadn't as Damon stopped beside her, his gaze zeroing in on her mouth.

'Would you like a drink?' He gestured to the bar.

'No. No, thank you.' That would only prolong the agony of waiting. Better to get this over before her craven urge to run sabotaged her intentions.

He stopped before her, eyebrows raised. 'No? So eager, Callie. I like that. I like it very much.' With one hand he tilted her chin so she met his ebony eyes. They gleamed with a heat that scorched her right to the soles of her feet in her high-heeled sandals. The stroke of his finger along her jaw evoked memories of pleasure she'd almost forgotten in her anger and distress.

Maybe...maybe this wouldn't be as hard as she thought. If he'd sweep her into his arms, kiss her with the same passion they'd shared once before, perhaps she could forget she was selling herself to him. That she had no choice.

But even as her eyelids fluttered in expectation of his next caress, his hand dropped and he stepped back.

What now? Why had he stopped?

'You want me to make this easy for you. Don't you, Callie?' The words hung between them as the silence lengthened.

Yes, she almost screamed at him, her nerves raw with the tension crawling through her. Please, please, just...

'But, given your condescension and your cold treatment, I think it's time you made the first move.'

Callie's jaw sagged and she snapped it shut as a surge of vibrant emotion straightened her weakening resolve.

'You want your pound of flesh, is that it?' She spoke through clenched teeth.

His lips twitched. 'You could say that, *glikia mou*.' His firm mouth, so beautifully sculpted, curled up into a smile that made her want to smash something. Preferably him.

'So what did you have in mind?' Already she dreaded the answer.

'You're my mistress now. I'm sure you'll think of something. Why don't you just seduce me?'

Seduce him! She had no idea where to start. When they'd made love there'd been little thought involved. It had seemed so natural, so right, she didn't remember a conscious decision to give herself to him.

Tentatively she reached out, screwing up her courage as she lifted her hand to his face. But she moved too late. Her hand touched air as he stepped away and sank onto a long sofa.

Nonchalantly he spread his arms along its back and stretched his long legs, crossing one ankle over the other.

'Go on,' he urged, for all the world as if he anticipated a show!

Did he expect a striptease? Wrath heated her chilled body at his deliberate show of power.

How like Alkis he was in his smug superiority. Something like hatred clawed at her chest, tightening her throat. But it helped. Now her hands were rock-steady as she jerked out the rhinestone pins holding her hair up.

Moments later her hair slipped down, a concealing weight around her shoulders and breasts. Callie let the pins fall.

'And the diamonds.' His face was unreadable but his voice sounded curiously thick. 'I don't want you coming to me wearing another man's diamonds.'

His proprietorial demand reinforced her contempt. He thought by possessing her body he had a right to control *her*. She unsnapped the bracelet and tossed it onto the marble coffee-table. Her earrings followed, splashes of scintillating light in the lamp-light. Callie raised her hands to the clasp of the necklace and caught Damon's look as it raked her face and upthrust breasts.

A shock of sensation jolted her out of her fury. A shock of something almost like excitement.

She dropped the necklace to the table and discovered she was breathing hard, as if she'd run here instead of tottering on ridiculously high heels. She stepped out of the delicate slingback sandals and her feet sank into the luxurious pile of the carpet.

Still he said nothing, just watched her with eyes that glowed with an inner fire.

No time for second thoughts. She'd committed herself. Head up, back straight, she paced towards him. He didn't move except to tilt his head, the better to watch her.

He really was a manipulative bastard. He enjoyed this power play. She sensed it even though his face remained granite-hard.

The realisation gave her the strength to sink onto her knees beside him on the sofa. She twisted a little, her leg aligning with his thigh, so solid and warm and unmoving. Without giving herself time to think she reached out and cupped his jaw in her hand. His skin was hot and smooth. So smooth she wondered if he'd just shaved. Had he been so sure she'd come to him?

Of course he had. He held all the cards.

Anger spurred her on. She leaned in and kissed him, full on the mouth. He didn't move. Didn't respond. His lips were warm and uncooperative. She tried again, this time pressing closer, her tongue flicking across the seam of his mouth. He didn't open it for her.

Callie clasped his face in both hands, caressing him slowly. She pressed kisses to the corner of his mouth, along his jaw and up to his ear, grazing her teeth along flesh that tasted of that unique spicy tang she remembered from a week ago. A shiver of pleasure, an echo of heady excitement, raced through her, tightening her skin. She inhaled his scent as she nuzzled his neck and a wave of dizziness hit her.

She edged closer, pressing herself to his solid heat. Her hands slipped down to the collar of his shirt, swiftly unbuttoning till she could slide her fingers, her hand inside. Crisp hair and steamy skin met her touch as she smoothed her palm across his firm pectoral muscles.

A dart of pure heat pierced her, arrowing straight to her womb, and lower, to the juncture of her thighs, as heady memories of sensual pleasure swamped her.

Again she kissed him, urging him, silently pleading with him to let her in. To reciprocate. This wasn't about his challenge any more. She felt that telltale surge of desire deep within her at the touch, taste, scent of Damon. It felt suspiciously like… coming home.

Despite her anxiety, her anger, her disappointment, there was a truth about this, about her and Damon together, that was more powerful than logic or pride. The realisation swamped her, flattening her defences.

Her trembling fingers worked frantically at the remaining buttons, ripping his shirt open to bare his torso. Callie sighed her pleasure as she slid down, exquisitely aware of the friction between their bodies as her breasts, covered only by thin silk, moved against his broad chest. Darts of fire lit the darkness behind her closed lids as she experienced again the raw power of sensual need.

She licked his collarbone, then swept urgent kisses down his sternum. He tasted as good as she remembered.

Following instinct, she licked one firm nipple, then tugged it lightly between her teeth. He shuddered and she let her questing hands mould and stroke the powerful contours of his chest. Did his heart beat faster? It pounded against her palm as she slid her arms round him.

He was so big, so superbly made that her pulse ratcheted faster in awareness of all that restrained masculine power. She remembered how he'd used that power so wonderfully, so tenderly to make her come alive in his arms.

Fire danced in her veins and need shimmered through her, drawing every nerve-ending awake and aware.

Callie rose, nipping his jaw, his chin, kissing his mouth with an insistent urgency that threatened to spiral out of control. She speared her hands through his thick hair, holding him captive as she teased, tempted and silently implored him to respond. That was what she needed, what she craved.

She sagged against his chest, breasts sliding against him. Sparks of pure delight flared from the contact. The heat built, urging her on.

Hurriedly she slid a hand to the waistband of his trousers, fumbling to undo his leather belt.

His mouth moved beneath hers. Yet he didn't return her kiss.

'At last,' he drawled. Callie sat back on her heels as his tone penetrated the haze fogging her brain. His glittering eyes held her captive.

'I thought you'd forgotten *I'm* the one you're supposed to pleasure. Not yourself. You'll have to improve your technique, Callie, or I might change my mind about having you. Perhaps I should take your little cousin as my wife instead.'

It was a douche of icy water, shocking her out of her stupor.

Callie's skin crawled as she realised what had happened. In a few short moments she'd forgotten everything about why she was here: his callous demand, her subservient role, the degradation of giving *herself* like a commodity in a business deal. Unbelievably all that had been obliterated by a force so strong it terrified her.

She'd succumbed to a primal, inexplicable need. The need for *him*. It shattered everything, even her pride, to smithereens. All that remained was a compulsion so strong even now she felt it pulse and rage in her blood.

She'd been completely out of control while he…

Shame and hurt and rage warred, forming an ice-cold lump of misery in her chest.

How had it happened? Through years of unhappiness, of occasional desperation, only control, her ability to withdraw inside herself, had kept her strong. It was how she had survived.

His hands thrust hers aside, making short work of his belt. Callie heard a zip slide down, then he spread both arms again along the sofa, the image of supercilious impatience. She scooped a lungful of air, transfixed by his arrogant stare.

In the gloom his expression looked familiar. The hard line of his mouth, the cold glint of his eyes. So had Alkis looked as he berated her for her failings, chastised her for not pleasing him in some way, or accused her of infidelity.

She'd escaped one manipulative man only to fall prey to another.

The searing, life-affirming heat of desire she'd felt seconds ago seeped from her body as ice-cold splinters of horror ripped through her.

What had she almost done?

Unbelievable that she'd hungered to give herself to this man! And all the while he'd felt nothing but impatience for her inexpert caresses.

Something shrivelled inside. If she did this, she'd lose what little was left of her hard-won self-respect. That was all she'd salvaged from the last six years.

In a surge of desperate energy she propelled herself back off the couch and onto legs that wobbled uncontrollably.

'Well?' He raised one interrogative brow. 'I'm waiting.'

She opened her mouth but no sound came. She slicked dry lips, ignoring the flicker of interest in his gaze. He sat with his clothes open, his arms splayed. He looked every inch the arrogant sensualist, awaiting his pleasure.

The thought nearly choked her.

Callie took a step back, then another.

'What are you doing?' The lazy boredom disappeared from his voice. His tone sharpened.

Fear spiked. Fear that, even now, she couldn't quite conquer the urgent desire that drew her back. Even arrogant and impatient Damon Savakis wielded a power that made her tremble with feminine weakness. That shamed her.

A second later Callie spun round and wrenched open the door. She grabbed her long skirts in her hands and raced pellmell up the path, terrified that at any second his hard hands would curl round her shoulders and yank her back.

Gravel bit her bare feet, her hair streamed behind her and a sob tore from her constricted throat. She stumbled but kept running, her breath sawing desperately in her throat.

She'd only just escaped the degradation of a loveless marriage to a venal, cold-hearted man. She *couldn't* deliver herself into the hands of another like him.

It was asking too much.

* * *

Damon stared in disbelief at the pale figure flying up the hill, long skirts billowing about her as she ran.

He stumbled to his feet, cursing his lack of co-ordination. He could no more catch her up than he could fly. His body was in lock-down, gripped in the stasis of a sexual arousal so potent it hurt to move.

Hell! It hurt to breathe.

Damn his vitriolic tongue. His need to assert his dominance.

Dominance! His mouth compressed in self-disgust.

He'd been putty in her delicate, sensual hands. Only determination to make her pay for her condescension, for the burning frustration he'd suffered, had lent him strength not to plunder her mouth and her body instantaneously.

Pride demanded he remain unresponsive to begin with.

He'd gripped the sofa so hard in his effort not to respond that his fingers were numb. The upholstery was probably shredded. She'd bewitched him and he'd fallen into a helpless state of immobility, muscles frozen in stunned disbelief.

Damon had reached breaking point. He'd been about to ravish her luscious mouth when she fumbled at his belt and relief spiralled through him. Just as well she hadn't touched him lower or he might have embarrassed himself. He was more explosively aroused than he'd been since his teenage years.

That realisation had given him the bare strength to meet her eyes and lie bald-faced about how she made him feel.

He'd never relinquished power to any woman. The realisation that she, of all women, had turned the tables with just her kisses and her slow caress of his bare torso, scared the hell out of him.

He'd lashed out, trying to redress the imbalance of power. Now look where that had got him!

Cursing himself for a fool, he did up his trousers and walked stiff-legged to the door. The winding path was empty. Callie was long gone.

Unbelievably, for the first time he could remember, Damon had overplayed his hand.

* * *

It was late when Callie emerged next day. After a night of no sleep she'd spent ages concealing her pallor and puffy eyes with make-up.

Had Damon left for Athens? Had he changed his plans and announced he'd marry Angela?

Callie bit her lip and faltered to a stop on the stairs. Her chest constricted, misery swamping her. She'd failed Angela. Guilt burned a hole in her belly.

Despite her determination, her vaunted self-possession, she'd let Damon frighten her into failure. It almost didn't matter that she'd pay a personal price now. He'd be furious enough to screw the Manolis family for every penny and she'd never get back what her uncle had stolen.

But that was only money. She'd find a way to pursue her dream, even if it meant years of delay. She *would* support herself and lay to rest the taunting echo of Alkis' voice telling her she was good for nothing but show. He'd belittled her brains, her ability and almost succeeded in breaking her. But she'd prove him wrong. Prove her worth to herself.

The thought of Angela, trapped in a marriage that would destroy her happiness, her very soul, ripped Callie apart. And her aunt, diagnosed with a heart condition, who'd lose her home if the deal didn't go ahead.

Callie had just discovered that bombshell this morning as she looked in on Aunt Desma. The results of the medical tests had come through. Her aunt put on a brave face, but the prognosis was serious. She needed quiet and professional treatment. Not to be uprooted from her home. Not to deal with her husband's volcanic temper if he lost everything.

It was the stuff of nightmares.

Guilt swirled inside her. She'd had the power to save them all, to placate the man who held their futures in the palm of his hand.

She'd failed them.

'Callista!' Her uncle's voice echoed up from the vestibule.

'There you are. Come here immediately. You're needed.' She peered over the railing to see him bustle back into his study.

Reluctantly she forced herself down the stairs. Was Angela's marriage a *fait accompli*? Or had Callie's actions last night scuppered the deal completely? If Damon was as incensed as she suspected, had he pulled the plug on the merger?

No, business would always come first with Damon. He wouldn't let a woman get in the way of profits.

Her uncle turned as she reached the doorway. His brow was puckered but his unctuous smile sent a shiver of revulsion down her spine.

Damon had done it, then—announced his intention to wed Angela. Callie's stomach cramped so violently she grabbed the door to hold herself upright against the pain.

'Come in, come in. It's time you turned up. We've been waiting for you.'

'For me?' She stepped over the threshold and slammed to a halt when she saw his companion, leaning back in an easy chair. Damon Savakis, large as life and wearing an impenetrable expression.

'Of course.' Aristides Manolis seemed ill-at-ease. 'Damon and I have sorted out the business side of things. But there are personal matters to be resolved.'

'Personal?' The word was torn from her lips. Surely that meant a wedding. Callie swung her head, searching for her cousin. The study was empty but for the men.

Damon's mouth curved in a slow smile. Something hot and possessive flickered in his eyes.

The door closed behind her with a snick that sounded like the clang of a prison door.

CHAPTER SIX

DAMON watched Callie's stiff posture and wary eyes.

Quite an act. She looked almost apprehensive.

As if she didn't know her uncle had spent the last hour haranguing him about his intentions, trying to manoeuvre him into 'doing the right thing' by the woman he'd compromised.

Disgust rose as Damon thought of their cleverly orchestrated ploy.

He'd been genuinely remorseful for his behaviour last night. There'd been no excuse, not even the confusing welter of emotions Callie created inside him.

After a lifetime protecting the women in his family he understood how appalling his behaviour was. He'd spent a sleepless night berating himself for arrogance, stupidity, his bloody ego. To distress her so...

He'd arrived at the house early, needing to see her.

That was when he'd learned the whole scene had been a charade. Manolis and his niece had set him up. *Again.*

Manolis had taken the tone of disappointed host and strict guardian. He'd seen Callie enter the house last night. She'd been distraught, he'd said, adding a reference to her dishevelled state, her lack of jewellery and shoes.

It was a new experience for Damon, being wrong-footed by his own actions.

A niggle of conscience reminded him that, as far as the world was concerned, he'd acted reprehensibly. Society's rules, his obligations as a guest, his own sense of honour all damned his behaviour.

Except Callie was no victim. Manolis had pulled out all the stops. Throwing his daughter at Damon in hopes of a marriage to secure financial security. And, as back-up, a dirty little scheme of blackmail. From the moment Callie had given herself to her tearful flight, it had all been a con to entrap him. She'd played the role of distressed victim last night.

Fury sizzled in Damon's veins. He'd never been so gullible. He should have been more cautious dealing with an unscrupulous old fox like Manolis.

Instead he'd let desire cloud his judgement. In that their cheap ploy had worked.

His pride screamed for payback.

Damon interrupted Manolis as he wittered on about resolving the situation. Damon would resolve it, but not the way this pair intended.

'I'll talk to your niece alone.'

Manolis objected but Damon cut him short.

'It's too late for a chaperone.' Damon met her snapping gaze and wondered if she'd ever been a naïve innocent. She was perfectly suited for the role of *femme fatale*. 'Your niece is a widow, not an inexperienced teenager.'

Callie shut the door carefully behind her uncle. She pressed clammy palms to the wood, trying to centre herself. Between her uncle's words and Damon's steely glare, she felt dazed and cornered, her pulse tripping unevenly.

'What game are you playing?' She swung round to confront Damon where he slouched in an armchair.

One eyebrow rose indolently and her fingers curled into fists. She longed to shatter his superior air.

'Game? You accuse *me* of playing games?' Never had Damon looked so remote, yet Callie knew what she'd heard.

'What's this about us marrying?'

Her uncle couldn't be serious. Just the words froze her blood.

Her stomach dived in distress. The sangfroid she'd clung to so desperately deserted her. She pushed away from the door and paced, unable to keep a lid on churning emotions.

'What's wrong, Callie? Having second thoughts? Or do you feel cheated I haven't grovelled on one knee?'

Callie couldn't imagine Damon grovelling. Yet the idea of him on his knees before her made her feel hot and unsettled. Abruptly she paced to the window.

'I want to know what you're up to!'

'According to your uncle I'm satisfying honour and obligation by making an honest woman of you.' His face was unreadable, his words sharp. Her eyes narrowed on his rigid shoulders and tight jaw.

'It was Angela you talked of marrying.'

'So it was.' His expression didn't alter.

Her hands curled into fists of frustration. 'You don't want to marry me! You said so.'

He crossed one leg over the other, surveying her as she paced the room. He said nothing.

'I'm not—'

'What? A virgin?' He smiled and instantly fire sparked in her veins. 'It's not a prerequisite these days. Besides, our sexual compatibility is proven.'

'There's more to marriage than sex!' She turned her back on his penetrating gaze and stalked to the window.

'Ah, there speaks the expert. Tell me, is that what held your previous marriage together? Sex?'

Callie spun back, her hair flaring around her shoulders. 'My marriage is none of your business,' she hissed as poisonous memories swarmed to the surface. It was as if he knew all her weak points and delighted in prodding them. With every challenge, every snide remark, he stripped her bare and vulnerable.

'You don't even like me,' she whispered, focusing on a point in the distance.

The walls pushed in. Claustrophobia choked her.

Marriage! To another controlling male! Over her dead body.

The sound of slow clapping jerked her round. Damon's mouth twisted in a jeering smile as he straightened.

'Congratulations, Callie. If ever you decide to work for a living you'd be a huge success on the stage. You got that distress and confusion just right.'

'What are you talking about?' Callie felt she was walking on sands that shifted beneath her feet.

'Your display of reluctance is a little overdone. I know you and your uncle concocted this plot to snare a rich man to salvage the family fortunes. But I refuse to fall in with your plot.'

Callie frowned. 'There was no plot.'

'Your uncle just happened to be in the right spot at the right time to see you looking the picture of compromised virtue?' His eyes flashed. 'Give me credit for some sense.'

Numbly she shook her head. 'I don't want to marry you.'

'Just as well. Marrying you is the last thing on *my* mind.' He spat the words as if tasting poison.

Yet as she watched his expression changed.

'But I want you, Callie.' His voice vibrated with repressed passion. The stark hunger in his eyes sent incendiary sparks through her tense body. 'And now I'll have you. On my terms.'

'Terms?' It was a strangled whisper.

'In my bed. But the stakes have just got higher.'

He *couldn't* want her if he believed that of her. 'I don't understand.'

'After the…inconvenience of your little farce, I've decided I want more than one night. You'll be my mistress, at my beck and call, for as long as I desire.'

The sizzle in his eyes gave a whole new meaning to the phrase beck and call. The breath whistled from her lungs as his intentions sank in.

'But my uncle—'

'What? He's old-fashioned enough to be distressed at the notoriety of his niece living as my mistress rather than my bride?' His dark eyes snapped. 'Tough. The pair of you should have thought of that before you tried to manipulate me.'

'I didn't—'

'Don't waste your breath, Callie. Those are my terms.' He steepled his hands under his chin. 'Accept them or face the consequences.'

Her limbs stiffened at the threat in his dark velvet tone. Her mouth dried. 'What consequences?'

Damon uncurled his body from the seat and paced towards her. Each deliberate step reinforced the sensation she was being stalked. Backed against the window, she had nowhere to run. Her hands splayed on the cool glass behind her.

'You think I'd let you make a fool of me then walk away unscathed? You're not that naïve. I can break your uncle like that.' The click of fingers near her ear made her jump.

'Refuse me and I ruin him in a hostile takeover. I owe the Manolis family *nothing*. On the contrary,' his lips flattened to a grim line, 'the Manolis debt to *my* family is too long outstanding.'

Callie's eyes widened at the burr of deep-seated anger in his voice. He sounded, and looked formidable. She couldn't doubt he meant every word.

'Or,' he continued, 'I could temper my annoyance by taking sweet Angela for myself and leave your uncle at least the appearance of dignity.' Damon thrust his head forward aggressively, obliterating her illusion of personal space.

'Either way you lose. Your dear departed husband didn't leave you more than a pittance and that's already gone. Perhaps he'd discovered you weren't an ideal wife.'

His sarcasm barely penetrated. Callie's stomach hollowed as memories crowded. Of Alkis' accusations and threats. Of the nightmare life she'd led, unable ever to satisfy her husband's expectations.

'You had me investigated?' He must have, to know Alkis

had left his money to his children by an earlier marriage. Callie had thought herself beyond outrage, but a new shaft of pain sliced through her. She felt violated, knowing some investigator had pried into her life.

Was there no end to this nightmare?

'Only a cursory report into your current assets,' he said as if invading her privacy was nothing.

'Well,' she drawled, summoning the last of her fading strength, 'that's all right, then.'

His bark of spontaneous laughter echoed round the room. 'I see we understand each other.' He placed one hand on the wall beside her head, blocking her in. His heat enveloped her; his warm breath caressed her forehead.

'The time for playing is over, Callie. Come with me now, today. It's your only choice.'

Panic gripped her as she felt her avenues of escape cut off. She had too much experience of ruthless men to doubt for an instant that Damon would deliver on his threats.

Last night she'd run, unable to give herself cold-bloodedly to him. But escape had been an illusion. She'd have to face even that mortifying ordeal. Her heart sank.

Callie shuddered at potent images of Damon demanding her submission, Damon making her body sing like an instrument tuned only to his touch.

At least Alkis hadn't possessed her body. But with Damon there'd be no escape, no privacy. Instinctively Callie knew she couldn't survive a long-term relationship with him. His will was too strong, her physical weakness for him like a Trojan horse planted deep within the last bastion of her defences. Who knew what damage her destructive craving would do to her fragile sense of independence and self-worth?

Her only hope was to keep this short-term.

Determination and weary acceptance seeped through her, strengthening her spine.

His face was close when she raised her head. So close her heart thudded as awareness rippled through her.

'I have your word you'll leave Angela out of this?'

'You have it.' A gleam in his eyes betrayed his pleasure. No doubt he was planning ways to enjoy her surrender. Callie repressed a shudder at the knowing, intent lick of heat in his gaze.

Her tongue was clumsy as she capitulated.

'Very well. You can have your revenge. I'll go with you.'

'I thought we were taking the big ferry.' Damon heard a thread of what sounded like anxiety in Callie's voice and shot her a look as a servant took their bags from the four-wheel-drive and went ahead.

In the shade of the pine grove her face gave nothing away. It was a stiff mask, leaving him to speculate on that tiny betraying quiver at odds with her appearance.

Yet nothing could dim his satisfaction. Ever since she'd given in to his ultimatum two hours ago, anticipation had sizzled in his blood.

He intended to enjoy this liaison to the full.

'Do I look the type to travel on crowded ferries?'

Callie's shoulders lifted in a tight shrug. 'It's either that or a helicopter to the mainland.'

'Why bother when I have my yacht? We can be private aboard *Circe*.'

Damon took her in slowly, from her blonde head to the white top, pale yellow trousers that cradled her neat curves and low-heeled sandals. She looked fresh and alluring in a way that had nothing to do with mercenary schemes. She looked...innocent.

His mouth thinned at the absurdity. She was an expert in playing up to male fantasies. Last night's charade had proved her anything but innocent.

She knew how to tease a man's libido. And his conscience.

He hadn't been privy to her conversation with Aristides Manolis this morning, but he'd heard her uncle's bellowed disapproval. Manolis was chagrined his plan to snare Damon in marriage hadn't worked. Seeing the barely contained fury in the older man's eyes later, Damon knew an unexpected admiration for Callie. No little innocent could handle such a bully. Callie was savvy and determined. Quite an operator.

'But…' She paused and gnawed on her lip. He zeroed in on the movement, heat building in his belly even as his brain filed away that surprising hint of nerves for later consideration. 'We'd get to Athens faster if we flew.'

'Who said I want to return quickly? I told my assistant to cancel my appointments.'

Damon's gaze travelled appreciatively down her slim body. They were near the place where they'd discovered exactly how much pleasure they could give each other. Memories rose hot and close, tugging at his control.

But he wanted the luxury of his own bed when he had her again. Despite his anger at her plot, it was desire not revenge that fired his blood now.

'I'm looking forward to a *leisurely* trip,' he murmured.

She blinked but said nothing.

He'd swear she'd been about to blurt something. Curiosity stirred. The idea of Callie saying anything unguarded intrigued him. Even in anger she gave little away. Except when she'd argued so passionately that he shouldn't marry Angela. Then he'd known for sure she was genuine.

'Isn't *Circe* up to your standards?' The yacht, just visible through the trees, was a rare vintage classic.

He'd spent a fortune refurbishing *Circe* to the most exacting standards of a man used to the best. Callie probably preferred an ostentatious cruiser over gracious lines and perfect craftsmanship. Her jewellery revealed a flashy taste rather than an appreciation of beauty.

'*Circe* is glorious. Only a philistine would think otherwise.' Callie shot him a look that mixed surprise and scorn. 'It amazes me that a man obsessed with takeovers and revenge recognises quality when he sees it.' She turned on her heel and headed away from him.

Damon surveyed her. The clench and release of her sexy bottom as she walked drew a sigh of appreciation.

'How you stayed married so long with your sharp tongue is beyond me, Callie,' he said to her retreating back. 'I bet you didn't make allowances for your husband.'

He paused, intrigued, as she stopped and slowly turned. Her face was set in lines of rigid hauteur, her body preternaturally still. Had he hit a sore spot?

When she didn't immediately respond he continued, surprised at his need to know more. 'Did you give him the cold shoulder too?'

'I've told you, my marriage is none of your business.' She drew herself up straight, perfectly erect, perfectly poised. So damnably perfect to look at it was hard to believe she was so conniving.

'Why don't you talk about it? Because you're ashamed of the way you treated your husband? Don't try to tell me you're sick with grief. You're not mourning him.'

She paced towards him. Fury flashed in her eyes.

'I suppose you'd prefer I dressed in black and retire quietly for the rest of my life.' Her lips curled in contempt. 'It must be upsetting to realise a woman can get on just as well without a man in her life.'

'You admit it? You weren't in love with him?' Triumph warred with disgust as he took in her supercilious expression. 'Is that why you don't use your married name? Why you reverted to Manolis? Because he meant nothing to you?'

Damon knew an insane desire to stamp his presence deep in her psyche, make her feel so much her life wouldn't be complete without him.

If possible the chill in her gaze deepened. Her eyes were glacial pools that would suck the heat and the life from a man unwary enough to venture there.

'You're not sentimental about keeping your husband's name?' he prodded. 'Or about the man who shared your bed for all those years?'

Damon waited for her excuses, but her mouth stayed fixed in an unyielding line.

She really was a piece of work.

'So,' he murmured, 'you didn't love him. Not surprising when he was so much older than you. He must have been, what, twenty years your senior? More?'

'Thirty-five.' Her lips barely moved on the words.

'Thirty-five years older than you.' Damon whistled. 'It must have been a challenge, summoning the enthusiasm to make love to a man so much older.' The image of Callie, sprawled naked and beautiful, letting some grizzled codger do what Damon had done with her, turned his stomach. Acid rose in his throat. 'Did you lie back and think of all his lovely money you could spend?'

Silence enveloped them. A stillness so thick he could almost reach out and grasp it. Yet she didn't move. Didn't even blink.

What would it take to unsettle her? He *knew* that behind the frozen façade was a flesh-and-blood woman whose physical passion matched even his.

'You know nothing about my marriage,' she said finally. 'You're not even original in your insults. There's nothing you can say about my marriage that hasn't been said before.' She looked as if she didn't give a damn. 'You don't know me,' she added.

'I know all I need to know. I remember in perfect detail. Every sigh, every moan, every passionate response. You couldn't get enough of me.'

Damon stepped near, raising his hand as if to caress her cheek, stopping with his palm centimetres from her skin. Static electricity sparked between them, tickling his hand and igniting his libido.

He watched her sway the tiniest fraction, as if drawn irresistibly to his touch. She felt it too, the tug of desire, stronger than ever. Satisfaction warmed his belly.

Soon he'd have what he craved. Then, when *he* was satisfied, he'd resume normal life, free of this net that bound him tight. Even his fury at the stunt she and her uncle had pulled barely mattered. All that mattered was the extraordinary intensity of his need for Callie.

Their gazes meshed then she stepped away, her face set in a frown of displeasure and confusion that did nothing to diminish her vibrant beauty. His hand dropped.

'You're fantasising, Kyrie Savakis—'

'It's Damon, remember?'

She shrugged, a jerky movement that told him all he needed to know about her awareness of him, of them.

'Contrary to what you think, not all women are placed in your path solely for your amusement.'

'You mean you have some other purpose?' he jibed. 'Apart from socialising, and shopping, and attending a charity function or two?'

His sisters would have his hide if they heard him, and his mother. But he was too busy watching her reaction to his deliberately outrageous comment to care. He was determined to make her lose her cool.

Eyes like jade daggers speared him. The confusion in her expression disappeared, swamped by indignation. For what seemed a full minute she glared, till he felt the heavy, anticipatory thud of blood pound through his body.

'Congratulations,' she said finally, inclining her head. 'You know,' she mused, her voice soft enough that he leaned forward to catch each syllable, 'you're everything I'd expect of an arrogant Greek tycoon. And then some. Thanks for warning me what to expect.'

Without waiting for a response she turned and strolled down the path, her casual gait deliberate provocation.

Damon felt emotion rise to the surface as he digested her words. He had to bite down hard to stifle a bark of appreciative laughter.

Little viper. Did she really think her words could sting him? Yet he had to hand it to her, she didn't back down or sulk when challenged. She'd looked him in the eye and told him what she thought. Did she know how appealing that was?

Damon's curiosity stirred, as well as his libido. The more time he spent with Callie the more she intrigued him. She might be shallow and conniving, but she had backbone and a gumption that appealed.

She was more than a sexy bed partner. She was an enigma he was determined to crack.

CHAPTER SEVEN

THE deck shifted beneath Callie's feet. Automatically she adjusted her stance to its gentle roll. It was second nature, like riding a bicycle.

That didn't stop the *frisson* of panic sliding down her spine. She fought to suppress it.

Damon thought her shallow and unprincipled. She refused to let him think her a coward too. Surely she could conquer this phobia till they reached the mainland.

Once she'd have revelled in being aboard a sleek beauty like *Circe*. She slid her hand along a lovingly polished surface. It felt familiar. Smelled like memories of long-lost summer afternoons. Nostalgia welled and with it piercing memories of a simpler time. When she had been loved and loving. When the future had seemed bright and beckoning. Before she'd learned about cruel obsession and manipulation.

'Alone at last.'

Callie jumped and swung round to see Damon watching her. Reflective sunglasses hid his expression.

Her uncle's staff were heading ashore after depositing their luggage and supplies.

'Wishing you were with them?' His voice was sardonic.

How she did! Instead she confronted twin horrors: her phobia of small vessels and giving herself to the cold demands of a man bent on stripping her pride and self-esteem.

Her lips tightened in a mirthless grimace. If this didn't kill her she must emerge stronger.

'Why don't you show me around?' If she kept busy maybe she could conquer the worst of her fear.

His eyebrows rose. 'Of course. Follow me.' He led the way to the stairs, peeling off his shirt. Bare-chested, he looked the way he had the first time she'd seen him. The sun lovingly glinted off toned olive skin that rippled with strength.

Callie's throat dried as she followed. If only he was the sort of man she'd first thought him—generous, teasing and tender. A man she could trust.

'Do you usually sail alone?' She forced the question, refusing to dwell on fantasy.

'No. Usually the *Circe* is full to the brim with family.'

'Your family?' Callie froze on the top step. He *couldn't* be married!

He turned but in the gloom at the bottom of the stairs she couldn't read his expression.

'I'm the eldest of five and the last to hold out against matrimony. There's usually someone wanting to come out with me. I'm even adept at stopping toddlers falling overboard.'

The ripple of unexpected amusement in his tone sent heat slanting through her. Callie had a vision of Damon wearing nothing but long swim shorts, cradling a dark-haired child in his arms. The image was unaccountably appealing. Maybe he was different with his family. Less driven, able to trust.

That was none of her business. Callie firmed her jaw and followed him, eyes widening at the luxury she found.

'It's stunning,' she breathed, pivoting to take in the elegant furnishings and state-of-the-art equipment. The interior was a stylist's dream, a harmonious marriage of old-world charm and modern functionality.

'I'm glad you approve.' Strangely, she detected no sarcasm. He'd removed his sunglasses and scrutinised her through narrowed eyes. She allowed herself the pleasure of absorbing her surroundings. How she'd love to be commissioned to fit out a yacht like this. Maybe one day, if her home-furnishing business really took off…

'The only complaint so far is my mother's. That I didn't put in an oven large enough for a triple batch of moussaka.'

'Your mother sails with you?' That didn't fit her perception of him as a ruthless tycoon, isolated by his self-importance, busy with business and seductions.

He shrugged and smiled. The first real smile she'd seen since the day they'd come together down by the shore. Its impact was like an incendiary flare deep inside.

'It's in the blood. I come from a long line of fishermen.'

'Then your father must enjoy sailing too.'

A stiffening of his body warned her she'd overstepped the mark. 'My father is dead.' The words rang with a cool finality that didn't brook further questions. 'Come. I'll show you the rest.'

Their few moments of unexpected truce were at an end. And with it Callie's momentary ease. Tension gripped her shoulders as she followed Damon.

Several hours later, watching the sun set across the liquid-silk Aegean, Damon was puzzled.

Callie had confounded his expectations. No sooner had she climbed aboard than she'd slipped off her sandals, obviously aware of the need to respect *Circe*'s timber decking. She seemed completely at home on board. He'd seen her slide her hand along the timber and brass fittings as if she too relished the vessel's superb craftsmanship.

He'd put her to work and she'd anticipated his instructions. She was no stranger to sailing. Real sailing. Not lounging on a floating resort.

Yet her usual grace was lacking, her movements cramped and stiff. Unease tugged his conscience but he'd stifled it, suspecting some new trick.

Now, with the yacht anchored in the lee of a tiny island,

Damon stretched. He hadn't seen her in an hour. She was below, preparing their meal.

Heat coiled in his belly as he strode across the deck.

The cabin was dim. She hadn't put on a light. He catapulted downstairs and strode through the lounge, intent on finding her.

His body thrummed a heavy, urgent beat. Food could wait.

No sound of her in the galley. Damon paused, frowning as he took in the food on the counter. She hadn't got far with her preparations. Would she insist they make for port so someone else could deal with the chore of cooking?

He stalked towards the other cabins and almost tripped.

She was huddled on the floor in the semi-darkness, her back braced against one wall, her arms wrapped around knees drawn hard into her chest.

'Callie?' His voice was a hoarse croak of surprise as fear spiralled through his gut.

Not by a flicker did she register his presence. Her eyes stared but she didn't see him. She seemed…cut-off. Foreboding speared him as he saw her faint rocking movement.

Something was very wrong.

He hunkered beside her, touching her hand. It was icy.

'Callie, what happened?' Urgency welled. That sightless stare worried him.

He raised his hand to her face. Her cheek was too cool, and wet with the tears that dripped unheeded from her chin.

Damon's chest clamped at the sight of such patent distress. This was no act.

Warmth. That was what she felt. Heat enveloping her.

She'd been so cold. From the moment Damon had casually declared they'd travel on his yacht. The chill crept in, spreading like a frost till finally she hadn't been able to pretend to be strong. Till icy fingers of fear and ancient pain wrapped around her heart and squeezed tight.

Callie had tried to be brave, forcing herself to climb on

deck and appear unaffected. Each movement had tested her
determination as she obeyed Damon's instructions and tried
to douse her rising panic at being aboard.

She hadn't set foot on a yacht since she was fourteen. Not
since...

Callie burrowed closer to the wondrous heat, needing it as
a starving man craved sustenance. If only she could blank out
the memories.

Vaguely she realised the cold had started long before the
sight of the yacht moored and ready to carry her onto the
treacherous sea. It had sunk into her bones years ago. When
Petro had used and betrayed her. When Alkis had kept her in
a travesty of marriage that excluded normal human interac-
tion.

She shuddered as pain ripped through her. The pain of loss
and betrayal. The hurt she'd bottled up so long.

'You're safe now. You're all right.' The low burr of words
penetrated the fog of her distress.

Safe. It sounded wonderful. The heat intensified, curling
around her. She sank into it gratefully.

A rhythmic movement lulled her body. Gradually her muscles eased, leaving a dull ache in place of screaming tension.
She felt heavy. Exhausted.

It took a long time for her to realise the soothing rhythm
was the caress of a hand, rubbing up and down her back. That
it echoed the thudding near her ear. A muffled heartbeat.

Damon.

With an enormous effort, like a half-drowned diver struggling to the surface, Callie broke through the enveloping stupor. She began to take note of sensations.

She was cradled in his arms, surrounded by the living heat
of solid muscle and bone. Her head was tucked in under his
chin. To her horror she realised she never wanted to move from
this cushioned comfort.

He smelt of sunshine and the sea, of the potent salty tang
of a virile male.

Callie sucked in a breath. He must have found her huddled where she'd cowered as her defences crumbled. She'd needed to catch her breath, regroup and strengthen herself to ignore the distress that had sideswiped her so devastatingly.

Nothing like this had ever happened before, even in her darkest days. Her pulse thundered at the idea of him finding her.

'Callie?' The hand at her back halted. After a pause it resumed its soothing motion.

She considered pretending not to hear. But she couldn't play the coward.

'Yes?' she whispered, her voice raw and thick.

A silent shudder rippled through his big frame and she heard him exhale. In relief or annoyance?

No doubt he'd come below anticipating their next bout of verbal sparring. Or perhaps the surrender of her body.

Dread carved a hollow inside her. She wasn't ready for that.

'What happened?' His voice was surprisingly gentle.

Reluctantly Callie opened her eyes. They were in the master cabin. She recognised the wide fitted berth they sat on and the brass-edged portholes high in the walls.

Her breath stopped and she jerked back in his arms, realising the implications.

His bed. His mistress. His pleasure.

That was why he'd come to find her, to consummate their arrangement. Despite her determination to deliver what she'd promised, Callie couldn't stop the instinctive kick of repugnance at the idea of a cold-blooded coupling as he'd demanded last night.

One long arm roped round her shoulders and hauled her close, fitting her to him again. His heat enveloped her, from his steely thighs beneath her legs to his powerful chest and shoulders supporting her.

'Nothing happened.' The words were slurred, her voice unfamiliar. She had the oddest sensation of distance, even from her own body.

'You usually sit on the floor for a good cry, do you?'

Sarcastic wretch! She hadn't cried in years. Callie searched for a tart rejoinder but her brain was too muzzy.

'What is it, Callie? What's wrong?' One large hand cupped her jaw, his thumb swiping tears from her chin, across her cheek. But there was nothing sexual about his gesture. It was simply…comforting. Her eyes flickered and her head lolled. His heart beating beneath her ear mesmerised her.

'Don't go to sleep on me now.' His hand firmed on her jaw.

'I'm not sleepy.' But she felt strangely lethargic. 'I don't know what's wrong with me,' she blurted out. The wobble in her voice horrified her and she tried to rise. He held her still with an ease that would have frightened her if she'd been thinking clearly.

'Did you injure yourself?' He paused, letting the words sink in. 'I couldn't find a wound.'

She found it easier to respond to his brisk, impersonal tone. 'No. Nothing like that. I just…'

'You just…?'

'You're going to have to tell me,' he added in a conversational tone when she said nothing. 'I'm not going anywhere till I get the truth.'

Callie's lips twisted. Much he cared for the truth. He preferred his own skewed view of people.

'Callie…' No mistaking the warning in his tone as he tilted her chin up. She jerked her face free, letting her hair, loose now round her shoulders, curtain her features. She stared across the cabin, fixing her gaze on a porthole.

'I…don't like yachts.' Callie felt a sliver of grim amusement at that bland explanation. She just had to get close to a vessel like this to become queasy with terror.

'You don't like them?' His voice gave nothing away. At least he'd dropped the sarcasm.

'I…avoid them.' Understatement of the century. For eleven years she hadn't been on anything smaller than a massive, multi-level inter-island ferry. Even that was a test of her nerves, leaving her shaken and sick to her stomach.

'You get seasick?'

She shook her head.

'Not seasick. So it's something else.' He wasn't going to let up till he'd prised the whole story from her. 'But you're a sailor, a good one.' Callie blinked in surprise at his praise. 'You didn't learn your way around a yacht by staying ashore.'

She hitched her shoulders. 'I used to sail as a kid.' Some summers she'd spent more hours on the water than ashore.

'And then?'

She dragged in a breath, knowing she couldn't escape this. He wouldn't let her go and he wouldn't settle for prevarication.

'My parents died when their yacht foundered in a storm off the coast north of Sydney.' Callie's view of the porthole misted but she kept her voice more or less steady. 'They'd gone to assist another craft in distress. In the end both yachts were lost.' A lump the size of the acropolis rose in her throat and she had to pause before continuing. 'There weren't any survivors.'

'How old were you?'

'Fourteen.' So long ago yet right now, aboard the gently swaying yacht so much like the one her dad had refurbished, the grief was as fresh as it had been then.

Maybe if their bodies had been recovered, if she'd been able to say her goodbyes instead of being whisked off to Greece by her uncle, who'd decreed that attending a memorial service would only upset her further...

'I'm sorry.' The simple, apparently sincere words, sliced through the silence. Callie turned to meet his eyes.

She'd expected impatience, derision even, at the childish fear she'd been unable to shake. Her uncle had no patience with her phobia. She was just thankful Alkis hadn't been aware of it, as he'd preferred flight to sea travel. Callie could imagine the vicious delight he'd have taken in exploiting her weakness.

But Damon's eyes held nothing but regret. She blinked, absorbing his sympathy.

'Thank you.' Callie tugged her gaze away, her breath an uneven gulp in her raw throat. She was perturbed at the illusion of warmth, of connection that sparked between them. Her emotional meltdown must have shorted something in her brain, making her imagine things.

'You should have told me before we came aboard.'

She shrugged. It hadn't occurred to her. Men, in her experience, didn't let a little thing like female nerves stand in the way of their plans.

How could she have known she'd react like this?

She'd thought she could master her fear. But the feel of the yacht beneath her feet had been the last straw after days strung out with tension. Damon's demands and manipulative methods had resurrected memories she'd worked hard to repress, of Alkis and their awful sham of a marriage. Of a misery so intense she'd thought she might die of it.

The extremity of her grief, welling up through her very pores, had stunned her.

'Why didn't you tell me?'

She turned. He looked sincere. But that meant nothing. She raised an unsteady hand, swiping tears from her cheeks.

Callie hated that he'd seen her so vulnerable.

'Why hand you one more weapon to use against me?'

Damon's lungs constricted as he read the sincerity in her drowned eyes. She meant it!

A splinter of pain pierced his chest as he watched her withdraw into herself again.

She thought he'd stoop so low? To use her genuine fear, her grief over her parents' death, to his own ends? It was one thing to play on her desire to keep her cousin from him, another to plumb such depths.

Shock tore through him.

He remembered the loss of his own father. Remembered too well its impact on his mother and siblings. The desolation and the grief. No decent man would use such emotions for his own gain.

Damon was a hard man in business, but honest. With women he was generous.

Pride revolted that Callie thought so little of him.

Suddenly this wasn't about the give-and-take game of awareness between a man and a woman. Callie referred to a different sort of battle. An ugly one with no holds barred.

What sort of men had she mixed with to make her believe he'd use her grief against her?

Her uncle was a selfish opportunist, but she'd faced him down only this morning.

Who else? Her husband? Men she'd known during her marriage? Had her lovers been so unsavoury? Had they used her in some way, rather than being fodder for her rapacious desires as he'd assumed? The notion stirred protective anger.

A sliver of doubt stabbed him as he thought of his ultimatum. The power he'd wielded to make her come with him.

It was something he'd never done before—threaten a woman into his bed. Logic told him he was simply turning the tables on her. She'd connived and now it was his turn. She was facing her just deserts.

Yet he couldn't repress a shiver that felt like guilt as she huddled in on herself.

'Come here.' His voice was rougher than he intended as he stripped the covers and lifted her onto the bed.

Wide eyes met his before she jerked her head away. Her mouth compressed in such misery his chest squeezed.

He swung her legs up so she lay in the bed. Seconds later he'd shucked off his shoes and lay beside her, drawing the covers over her. He slid his arms around her and pulled her close so her head rested on his collarbone.

She needed warmth and comfort.

Something other than his libido surfaced as he cradled her. He wanted to take care of her.

He'd feel the same about anyone in these circumstances.

Callie lay rigid in his arms.

After an interminable time she moved. Fingers tickled his throat and he swallowed down the surge of need that threatened to swamp him.

This was no time for sex.

Then he realised what she was doing. She'd fumbled his top shirt button open and was working on the next, her hands a delicious torment on his over-heated skin.

'Stop!' He clamped his palm over her hand and reared back so he could see her properly.

She was pale, her eyes enormous in her tear-washed face. Even her lips were pallid. But she'd stopped crying and there was a determined set to her mouth.

'What are you doing?' he demanded.

Her gaze slid to where he held her captive. Only now did he register the fine tremor in her fingers. He stroked them with his thumb, aware of their fine-boned fragility.

'Delivering on my promise.' Her voice was a husky wisp of sound, barely audible.

'Your promise?' He frowned, his mind still grappling with the evidence of her vulnerability and his body's inevitable response to her tentative caress.

'I promised myself to you. As your mistress,' she added as if she hadn't been clear the first time. 'You wanted—'

'I know what you promised,' he growled, thrusting her hand away as if stung. The reminder of their agreement, now, with her so patently vulnerable, made their deal seem tawdry.

Surely she couldn't believe he'd demand she give herself here, now, when she was in such a state.

Surprised eyes met his. Grimly he tugged her close, pulling her head down to his shoulder. So he didn't have to look into those bruised green depths.

Heat scorched him from the soul out. Guilt engulfed him.

'Close your eyes and sleep, Callie. This isn't the time.'

CHAPTER EIGHT

'You have a beautiful home.' Callie gazed across the broad curve of the horizon pool to the indigo sea and the darker bulk of the mainland beyond. The peace of the tiny island enveloped her. After the shock of her emotional meltdown yesterday this was balm to her soul.

If only she could be alone to enjoy it.

Her skin prickled and she knew he watched her. Reluctantly she turned. He sat just a metre away.

His eyes snared hers and remarkably she felt again the illusion of connection with him she'd experienced the first time.

'I'm glad you approve. I didn't think it would be to your taste.'

His gesture encompassed the mansion behind them. Not a modern construction as she'd expected but a lovingly restored home with a history of its own. It had elegant long windows, full-length shutters, a pantiled roof and delicately poised balconies. Inside, as on his yacht, Damon had blended grace with modern convenience.

Callie's gaze followed the line of the house to an unfinished building in a similar style, connected by a glazed walkway that surprisingly worked, rather than detracted from the original villa.

Damon was expanding, using the centuries-old house above its private bay as his centrepiece.

Callie liked his approach.

'Just like you assumed I wouldn't like the *Circe*?'

'My mistake.'

Callie blinked. In years of marriage she'd never once heard Alkis admit to an error. Even to something so trivial. She grimaced and swallowed some wine. It slid like nectar down her throat. Only the best in Damon's home.

'My uncle's taste isn't mine.' He probably thought she'd inherited Aristides' love of over-the-top decoration.

Just as he'd assumed she was conniving and unscrupulous like her uncle.

'So I'm discovering.' Damon's gaze slid over her, taking in her simple, stylish dress in cream and bronze. The colours suited her but there was no cleavage on display.

She lifted her chin. 'Disappointed?'

'Intrigued.' The banked heat in his gaze revealed a familiar hunger. And something more: curiosity.

No wonder. He'd got more than he bargained for when he took her aboard his yacht. She cringed at the memory of that episode. He'd seen her at her most vulnerable. Yet to her amazement he hadn't taken advantage of that.

Callie had woken from a dreamless sleep this morning to find Damon had sailed overnight to the mainland and organised a helicopter flight to his island.

He'd saved her the distress of staying on his yacht. When she'd tried to thank him he'd brushed aside her gratitude as if he'd done nothing at all!

More, he'd rejected her fumbling attempt to initiate intimacy. Instead he'd simply held her till she slept. The memory of his steady heartbeat soothing her, his strong arms protecting her, his scratchy chin moving against her hair as he spoke, created a tiny unfurling bud of warmth deep inside her.

There'd been no chastisement for her weakness, no rant about the inconvenience she'd caused. Instead she recalled his brusque tenderness as he'd rocked her to sleep. Damon had been patient and practical, as if dealing with a mistress's phobia were commonplace.

She couldn't fathom him, morphing from cold-blooded manipulator to carer in the blink of an eye. She'd never have believed it possible.

Who was Damon Savakis, really?

'Is your family from this island?' The intensity of his stare unnerved her. Polite conversation was better than silence when he watched her every move.

At least watching was all he'd do, for now. This morning she'd had to explain, red-faced with embarrassment, that her monthly cycle had begun early. Damon hadn't batted an eyelid, no doubt used to such discussions with live-in lovers.

She didn't have to please him in bed. Yet.

'No, we're from the south. From the Peloponnesus.'

'So why here?' Nerves forced her to continue.

He shrugged and she was reminded of him, bare-shouldered onboard *Circe*. Heat rippled through her and she looked away.

'I'd sailed here and knew the island. It's an easy commute to Athens by chopper or even speedboat.'

'You travel every day?' He'd left her here all day, alone but for his unobtrusive staff. Presumably he'd spent the time working, despite his plan to take a few days off.

Of course, that was before he'd learned his new mistress was inconveniently unavailable for sex.

Why spend time here in the meantime? Nothing could have reinforced more clearly her place in his world. She served just one purpose.

'This is a holiday retreat. My principal home is in Athens. But I thought you might appreciate the peace here.'

Just like that Damon pulled the rug out from under her assumptions. He'd come here so she could recuperate?

Heat flushed her throat and cheeks. Mortification warred with gratitude and surprise. 'I... Thank you. That's very kind of—'

'Besides,' he spoke again, cutting off her clumsy thanks, 'I wanted to check how the build was progressing.' He gestured to the extension beside the original villa.

Callie pressed her lips together. Either he didn't want her thanks or she fitted neatly with his existing plans. She had no idea which. With Damon all her certainties crumbled.

'I make it a point to keep a personal eye on all important matters.'

'Like visiting my uncle when you took over his company?' The words were out before she could regret them.

'Precisely.' Damon's mouth firmed as he watched the distant view.

'Do you oversee every deal?' He was a billionaire with a reputation for decisive action. Surely he delegated some negotiations to his staff.

'Ah, but that was more than a business deal.' His lips twisted in a grim smile. 'That was personal.'

'How?' As far as she knew her uncle had never met Damon before this week.

Slowly he turned to face her. His expression made her quiver. 'He didn't tell you.' It was a statement, not a question, almost as if he spoke to himself. 'Both my grandfather and father worked in the Manolis shipyards.'

Callie felt the slide of premonition down her backbone, like the touch of an icy finger.

'My father died in an industrial accident there.' He spoke in a monotone. But she saw the angry glitter in his eyes.

'I'm sorry.'

Again that shrug of wide, powerful shoulders.

'Your uncle was in charge of the company by then and his lawyers saw to it my mother didn't get compensation. She barely got enough to cover funeral costs.'

Callie gasped at such callousness. But she could believe it of her uncle. He was all for screwing money out of the business any way he could. Empathy for workers was a foreign concept to him.

Remorse stabbed her, carving through her chest.

With his action Aristides had tainted the company her father had helped expand. He'd tainted their family. No wonder Damon expected the worst of them. Of her.

'Acquiring Manolis Enterprises was payback. Is that it?'

Silently he nodded.

'How long have you been planning your takeover?'

'Since the day the lawyer bullied my mother into relinquishing her claim for compensation.'

Silence stretched, a taut wire between them.

All this was about revenge? Even his pursuit of her? Carefully she placed her glass on a nearby table as her hands began to shake. Her pulse pounded frantically.

How better to triumph in his victory over her family than to rub their noses in her weakness for him? No wonder he'd targeted her for seduction. She'd been collateral damage in his quest for vengeance.

The tentative warmth and gratitude she'd begun to feel leached away in the face of his calculating actions.

'You don't really want me,' she whispered. 'You want retribution.'

His ebony eyes gleamed as he surveyed her.

'Wrong, Callie. I have my payback. But make no mistake. I want you too.'

Eight days later Damon emerged from the pilot's seat of his chopper and strode from the helipad to his villa.

As usual, he was eager for his first glimpse of Callie.

Today the business with her uncle had been finalised. Contrary to his original plans, Damon had settled a generous sum on Manolis. The memory of Angela's tentative smile, the knowledge of Callie's worry for the sick aunt she rang daily, had played on his conscience. Instead of stripping the family bare of assets he'd acceded far more than he needed to.

He grimaced. He was getting soft.

His family told him his protective instincts were too strong, that he took his responsibilities for their welfare too seriously.

Now he found himself going out of his way to provide for his arch rival's womenfolk!

But the worry pleating Callie's brow whenever she got off the phone, her obvious concern for her relatives, touched him. In that she was genuine and he respected her for it.

Besides, Angela and her mother shouldn't suffer for Manolis' behaviour. Hadn't Damon slaved for years to protect his mother and siblings from the fallout of that man's machinations?

Strange how, after years plotting revenge, the reality was tempered by other considerations.

Yet he was satisfied with his decision.

He'd even decided to salvage what was left of Manolis Industries, building it into his own vast enterprise so it became profitable once again. Only a fool would destroy something with such innate potential.

He pushed through a side-door and bounded up the stairs, anticipation firing his blood.

He hadn't seen Callie since dawn, when he'd held her close and done nothing to assuage the ravening hunger to possess her again. For over a week now he'd kept his distance, insisting only that she share his bed. He had no intention of letting her establish herself in another room.

Each night had been a torture of thwarted desire, but he refused to give up the pleasure of sleeping with her. Even though he did precious little sleeping!

Her reaction aboard *Circe* had stunned him. He hadn't realised her vulnerability.

Nor had he counted on the twinge of guilt that assailed him about his tactics in getting her to himself. Despite the underhand blackmail stunt she'd organised with her uncle, he had a sneaking idea he'd lowered himself to their level in forcing her hand.

Yet grief for her parents didn't absolve her of how she'd lived since she was old enough to sell herself to a rich old husband. Or try to trick Damon into marriage.

She was simply more complex than he'd supposed, her mercenary gloss hiding doubts and fears, like anyone else.

Nevertheless, as he entered the corridor at the top of the stairs, he knew he wanted more. He didn't want Callie giving herself because he demanded it. Because he'd blackmailed her by playing on her fears for her cousin.

He wanted her to come to him because she wanted him.

He reached the door to the master suite and he heard running water. Damon slammed to a stop.

His groin hardened as his imagination presented a picture of Callie in glorious detail. Her hair would be like dark honey, slicked over her shoulders and down the sweet arch of her spine. Her thighs, belly and breasts glistening with water. Her hand moving slowly, soaping tender, sensitive skin.

A groan of anticipation filled his throat.

Damon reached out and turned the door handle.

CHAPTER NINE

CALLIE secured the plush bathrobe at her waist then bent to towel-dry her hair.

These last eight days in the luxury of Damon's private estate had given her plenty of time to think. Yet thinking got her no further forward.

She hated the way he'd forced her into this arrangement. Yet she'd seen glimpses of a better man hidden beneath the surface. A man who, despite every expectation, had gone out of his way to look after a woman he saw as his enemy when she was in distress.

The size of the Manolis family debt to his weighed heavily on her conscience. She could even understand, after dealing with her uncle, how Damon believed she'd tried to trick him in a plot to secure a wealthy bridegroom.

And running beneath all her ponderings lay the swift, dark channel of desire. Strong as rushing water, deeper than she cared to test. It blindsided her too often, especially when Damon held her in his arms every night, spooned in front of him or nestled across his chest. Each morning she'd wake to find they'd snuggled closer in sleep. His thigh between hers, his hand on her breast, her mouth on his warm throat.

Horrified by the way her body accepted his, she feigned sleep till he got up to shower ready for the office.

But nothing stopped the memories of a time when his touch had been magic to her starved senses.

When the time came and he demanded sex, would she resent his domination? Or would she welcome it?

Her indignation and defiance had wilted. Or was it just that today's news had sapped her strength? After a long discussion with her lawyer there was still no news of the trust. Her plans to start her business were indefinitely on hold. She couldn't rely on her uncle to hold to his promise.

Callie gritted her teeth and rubbed her scalp harder.

No! She wouldn't give up. She *would* make her new start. As soon as she was free of Damon she'd find herself a job and start saving. She—

Callie's hands stilled, tightening like claws against her scalp. A pair of large, bare masculine feet appeared in her line of vision.

Her heart pumped faster and her breasts rose and fell as her breathing turned shallow. The movement reminded her that beneath the towelling robe she was naked. Her skin contracted in shivery awareness of her vulnerability.

Adrenalin shot into her bloodstream. Suddenly every nerve was on alert.

Slowly she lifted her head. Dark trousers, superbly fitted over long, powerful legs, planted wide in an attitude of assurance. Pockets bulged where his hands rested, obviously at ease. Trim waist, flat stomach. A powerful chest beneath a tailored shirt.

Callie's heart nosedived as she saw the top buttons of his shirt open, his tie missing and the taut, anticipatory smile on Damon's beautifully sculpted lips.

His eyes blazed heat that spilled over her, stoking her temperature till her cheeks were on fire.

You're mine.

No need for words. His proprietorial expression said it all.

The towel dropped from Callie's nervous fingers and she bent, scrabbling to pick it up.

He stepped towards her and she backed, holding the damp towel in front of her, a token barrier.

'You're home early.' Her voice was a nervous whisper that matched the rising panic deep inside.

She'd told herself she'd go through with this, no matter how cold and demanding he was. He couldn't damage her pride any more than it had already been savaged. At least his arrogant demands would help her retain her contempt.

But there was a vast difference between theory and reality. Try as she might she couldn't conjure the cool persona she needed to keep him at bay.

Or silence the voice inside that purred in expectation of his caresses.

The reality of Damon in the flesh, a threat and a promise, sent her pulse skittering.

'Yes.' His eyelids lowered, giving him a sensuous look that made Callie's limbs grow heavy. 'I wanted to see you.'

Her eyes widened as he opened the cuffs of his shirt.

'I've been thinking about you all afternoon.'

His voice dropped to a deep, ultra-masculine burr of sound that made the fine hairs on her arms stand up. Her nipples peaked and she crossed her arms as if that would prevent her reaction.

'I…wanted to see you too,' she blurted, following the dexterous path of his long brown fingers as they flicked open every shirt button.

He raised one brow. 'Really?'

'Yes. My things have arrived. The belongings I left at my uncle's.'

He nodded then shrugged out of his shirt, tossing it onto the linen basket.

Callie tried to focus on the fall of fine silk, but her gaze swung back to Damon. His chest was bare: tanned, muscled, perfect. At the sight of his naked torso her stomach coiled tight and hard. She saw the fuzz of dark hair spread across his pectorals and arrow down his belly and remembered the feel of it teasing her nipples as they'd rocked together, moving as one.

'There's quite a bit of stuff,' she choked out, looking away, holding herself rigid. 'I haven't got a home base yet.'

She no longer had a home in the US and her uncle had refused to store anything of hers. He was furious that she'd stymied his plans for a Manolis-Savakis marriage.

'That's OK.'

Damon stepped closer, his hands at his belt. Callie backed up till she felt a wall against her spine.

'It's all been put in the bedroom at the far end of the hall. I thought—'

'I said it's OK. Keep your things there as long as you like. You can use that room as your own.' He paused. 'Except that you'll sleep with me.'

The flash of fire in his eyes confirmed he wasn't thinking about sleep. His expression made her defences crumble on their foundations.

Callie had an awful feeling if she let him close now she'd never be able to erect another barrier between them. The force of his personality was too strong.

'Do you want the shower?' she babbled. 'Let me just put this towel back then I'll get out of your way.'

Callie turned and stumbled to the towel rail, berating herself for her lack of coordination. Her prized composure, even her determination not to show any weakness, had deserted her.

Blood pounded in her ears as she fumbled to hang the towel over the rail. Finally she managed it then tightened the belt of her robe, assuring herself it was secure.

She was turning to leave, desperately searching for something, anything to say that would distract Damon from sex, when a sound made her freeze.

Running water.

Callie spun, then reached to grope for the rail as shock rippled through her.

Damon leaned into the massive double shower, adjusting the temperature of the spray. He'd stripped off the last of his clothes. He was completely, breathtakingly naked.

From this angle Callie saw the long sweep of his back and the heavy weight of his shoulders and muscled biceps as he reached for the taps. His thighs were solid, muscled and powerful. His buttocks tightly rounded.

She stood, rooted to the spot, unable to shift her gaze.

The solid planes and curves of his body made a magnificent picture.

She'd forgotten just how breathtaking he was. But her body hadn't. She felt the telltale softening between her legs, the anticipatory buzz of awareness, the revving heartbeat and knew she had to escape. Fast.

For, she finally realised, it wasn't Damon Savakis she feared. It was her own treacherous frailty.

He made her respond to him in ways she'd never dreamed possible, made her feel—

'Callie.'

His voice stopped her as she sidled to the door. It was a velvet promise of pleasure that tugged her eyelids to half mast and weighted her unsteady legs.

Just that one word weakened her resolve!

He stood before her, naked and unashamed. Fully, gloriously aroused, Damon Savakis was something to behold.

Callie's knees trembled as she stared. There was no escape. The faint scent of musk made her nostrils flare in the damp air. From his skin or hers?

Dark eyes scorched her mouth, her throat, everywhere they roved.

Her gaze dropped as he reached for something, a packet. He tore the corner and, eyes never leaving hers, fitted a condom, his movements quick and assured.

There was something incredibly erotic about seeing him, proud and ready for her. A surge of excitement scudded straight to her womb and tingles erupted deep inside.

His gaze claimed her. The melting warmth of her body was proof that physically she was his. He'd imprinted himself on her, awakening longings and desires she'd shelved long years ago. Now those longings centred on Damon.

Panic pulsed. Would she always feel this answering tide of hunger when he looked at her?

It wasn't the calculating stare that chilled her to the bone. It was the warm, smoky invitation she'd read in his eyes that first time. An invitation to pleasure…and something even more powerful that lured her, heedless of everything but the need to respond.

'Callie.' The word whispered through her, tugging at her senses. He reached out and took her tie belt in his hand, yanking so the material fell away.

A hiss of breath sighed in her ears as he watched her robe swing loose.

He stood as if frozen.

Callie experienced a surge of impatience. Why didn't he follow through? Touch her? Claim her?

Callie tried to summon indignation, outrage at being made to give herself to him. But nothing came. Only a buzz of excitement at the prospect of intimacy with Damon. It was just as it had been the first time.

Magical.

'Do you want this?'

It took long seconds before she made sense of his words.

'Callie. Do you want me?'

He was *asking* her? No hint of force. Just the compulsive pressure of her own desire.

Damon was handing her the power to say no. Making it *her* decision!

Callie swallowed a sob as contradictory, unexpected feelings overcame her.

Tomorrow she'd regret this. But right now the honest truth was she wanted this as much as he. It felt as if she'd always wanted this, wanted him.

'Callie!'

He stepped back, his face paling as his hands clenched at his sides. She almost cried aloud at his retreat.

With difficulty she swallowed a knot of welling emotion.

'Please.' Her voice was a mere croak of sound. 'Yes.'

That was enough. Instantly he stepped close, palming the heavy robe from her shoulders so it puddled at her feet.

His eyes blazed, fever-bright, as he raked her from head to toe. Instinctively Callie crossed an arm across her breasts and another down over the juncture of her thighs.

But she no longer felt modest. No longer felt like the person she'd known for the last twenty-five years.

Damon had changed her irrevocably.

His knee nudged her thighs as he backed her into the warm shower, his hands sliding to her wrists then skimming up to her shoulders. Excitement sparked where he touched, exploding with an intensity that snatched her breath.

This felt so right.

'Damon.' Even under the steady thrum of water, her hair plastered to her ears, the word sounded like a plea. Needy and bewildered. Callie reached out and clasped his slippery shoulders, needing support. More, needing to touch him with a desperation stronger than anything she'd known.

She craved his strength, his power, his ability to satisfy the hunger that devoured her so completely.

There was no thought now of compulsion or blackmail. This was as simple, as elemental as desire between a man and a woman could be.

'Glikia mou.' Damon nuzzled her neck, her collarbone, and shock waves tore through her, making her body jerk and tremble beneath his touch.

'I want you.' There was freedom in the words. A freedom she'd never expected.

Callie slipped her hands across his shoulders to his slick hair, clamping her fingers against his skull and drawing him down towards her.

Bliss as he opened his mouth to her. His lips moved sensuously. His tongue laved the inside of her mouth, caressing and teasing and satisfying with slow, erotic strokes. Long, hard fingers bracketed her cheeks and jaw, holding her still as he tilted her face for better access.

Callie's eyes closed. In the rich darkness colours exploded as their kiss grew from languorous to hungry. From hungry to desperate. Damon's chest crushed her so exquisitely she rubbed against him, revelling in the slippery friction.

Deep in his throat Damon growled and slid his arms round her, holding her still. His tight embrace was perfection.

She felt him everywhere, from his tongue, warm and seductive against hers, to his hand clasping her bottom, drawing her higher so her soft belly pressed against his steel-hard erection.

Heat coiled and she melted, butter-soft and ready for him. Her fingers slid through his wet hair, seeking purchase as she pressed close.

'Damon, please.'

She needed him.

Water sluicing on her breasts and belly made her eyes snap open. Damon still held her but he'd stepped away, allowing the spray to cover her. Callie reached to pull him close, beyond caring that it was her doing the begging.

Obsidian eyes met hers and she dragged in a breath as shock ripped through her. She barely recognised the man before her. His face was stripped bare of softness. The stark angles of his bones, the rigid line of his jaw and the inky black slash of his brows painted a portrait of raw hunger. Of a need that matched her own.

Callie's heart squeezed for the pain mixed with pleasure she read there. Instinctively she reached to cup his face, to offer the comfort of a kiss, but he moved too fast.

One moment he was there, staring down with the eyes of a tortured man. The next he'd dropped to his knees, hands spanning her waist as he suckled her left breast.

Her moan of ecstasy shuddered through the cubicle as he drew out pleasure so sharp she thought she'd faint. She cradled him, arching forward to meet his lips, his tongue, his teeth. Delight speared her and she shook, grateful for the wall at her back, hands propping her up.

Then he moved once more, nipping tiny erotic bites at her waist and belly that sent flashes of electricity jagging through her. Callie's head thudded against the tiles as weakness invaded her very bones.

Too late she realised his intentions. Broad hands pushed her thighs apart. Her eyes widened as she felt his hot breath between her legs.

'No!' Her head jerked forward and she met his arrested gaze. 'Don't.'

For a moment her brain seized, absorbing the sight of him there, kneeling like a supplicant before her. Heat twisted in her chest and her heart thundered.

'No?'

She shook her head, her hands pushing at his shoulders. Her reaction was purely instinctive.

'I don't…' Her words petered out under his unwavering stare. How gauche she must seem in her inexperience. 'I haven't ever…'

His gaze seared hers as the water cascaded around them, drumming on the tiles. His expression was unreadable.

'Then allow me.' He waited only a second for her response but it stuck to the roof of her mouth, like her tongue.

Then it was too late. Damon leaned in and nuzzled her in that most secret place. Sensations assailed her: sharper, more acute than she'd ever experienced.

Callie's fingers curled into claws as his tongue flicked out and traced a fiery path of ecstasy right at her core. She shuddered and clung to him, dazzled by the intensity of what he made her feel. Again and again. She couldn't breathe, couldn't think. Could only sag back against the tiles as rivulets of fire burned through her, igniting the most exquisite reactions. She'd never dreamed…

'Damon. Please…' Her keening cry choked into silence as,

like a red-hot lava flow, the momentum of pleasure built to an unstoppable surge.

Her knees gave way as sensation exploded, racking her body with wave upon wave of delight.

She shuddered and collapsed, sated and trembling as after-shocks of pleasure reverberated again and again. Her mind was a dazed whirl at this stunning new experience. At the gift he'd given her.

Hazily she was aware of Damon moving, holding her close, his solid body warm against hers. She sank against him, bone-less in his embrace.

'Thank you,' she whispered against his broad shoulder as another aftershock hit her. Her words were slurred.

'It was my pleasure.' His voice was a deep rumble she felt through her chest as he held her to him.

But he didn't let her sink into oblivion. A moment later the suck of his mouth on her nipple shot exquisite pleasure through her, echoing the pulse of her fading climax. She jerked in his arms, zapped by a jolt of electrical current.

'And it's not over yet,' he said as his hands circled her waist and lifted her off her feet.

Callie's eyes snapped open as she felt slippery tiles at her back again. She looked down into fever-bright eyes, a furrowed brow and a mouth drawn in a tight line of concentration. She barely had time to register that she was no longer standing when he stepped close, under her.

'Lift your legs,' Damon ordered in a hoarse, unrecognisable voice.

Gripping his shoulders, Callie complied, her knees encir-cling his hips as he lowered her, with excruciating slowness, till they joined.

Her breath stopped on a gasp of astonished delight.

She'd thought herself sated. Yet even that lightning bolt of ecstasy hadn't satisfied her as this did—the two of them to-gether as one, inextricably whole.

Callie leaned in, wrapping him closer. She was open to him

and part of him so completely. Emotion welled, filling the hollow place where fear and defiance and loneliness had resided so long. She wanted to please him as he had her. She wanted to give him—

The abrupt, urgent rocking of his body against hers blasted thought from her brain. Instinctively she clung tight, curving herself round him to counter and enhance each hard thrust. His hands slid down to clamp her hips and he sank his teeth against her neck in a tender bite that sent rockets of heat corkscrewing into her veins.

Callie's eyes were closing as a shadow of movement across the room caught her eye. In the far mirror wall she saw Damon, all superb male power, his buttocks clenching with each upward surge. His biceps huge and solid as he held her. Pale legs encircled his dark skin, pale fingers grasped his wide shoulders.

Together they looked...they looked...

One final potent thrust and the conflagration engulfed them both.

A roar of triumph rent the air. Damon pulsed urgently within and her muscles contracted hard, welcoming and encouraging.

Sensation erupted as she rode the powerful wave of pleasure with her lover.

She clasped him close, their hearts thundering together, completion shuddering through them, binding them as one. Callie knew moment after moment of purest joy, then awareness began to slide and she slumped against him.

Eventually, dimly she became aware of the drumming sound ceasing, of the pounding water ending. Still she clung to him, not wanting to dispel the magic encompassing them.

Gentle hands, strong hands moved against her. Plush, warm towelling enveloped her. A voice murmured in her ear, drawing her back to reality.

'Relax your legs, Callie.' Firm pressure forced her to unlock her ankles and let her legs slip down. Taut muscles groaned at the release of pressure and she trembled.

Her feet touched the ground but she couldn't stand. She was sinking out of his hold when powerful arms scooped her high against a chest that still thundered, like her own.

'I'm sorry,' she mumbled. 'I can't seem to—'

'It's all right, *Callie mou*.'

She lifted weighted lids to see Damon watching. He wore an expression she barely recognized: tenderness mixed with puzzlement. And more that she was too weary to comprehend.

Her lips curved as rare peace filled her. She turned her face into him. Her palm rose to the slick warmth of his chest.

Then the world slipped away and all Callie's cares with it.

CHAPTER TEN

CALLIE woke alone.

It was early morning, judging by the light rimming the curtains. She swept the bed with her hand. It was warm from Damon's body. His spicy scent mingled with the musky fragrance of sex, making her weak, remembering.

Emotion catapulted through her, feelings so potent yet so jumbled they barely made sense. Through the long night they'd been lovers. To her overwrought senses, her befuddled brain, it seemed *lovers* was the right word. That they'd shared more than mere sex.

There'd been tenderness, a generous warmth that had transported her back to that magical afternoon on the island, when the whole world had seemed brighter because of Damon. When for the first time everything had seemed *right*.

Was she fooling herself again?

Callie forced drooping eyelids open, as if morning light could oust the fantasies lingering after a night of bliss.

She ached in places she'd never before ached. Her body was replete, her limbs heavy. Yet energy zinged in her veins as never before. She wanted to leap out of bed and dance, to climb a mountain top and shout her joy.

In Damon's arms she'd felt...cherished.

Callie stared at the indentation on the empty pillow beside hers. What did it signify?

Her burgeoning happiness fizzled as if doused in cold water.

It didn't take a genius to work it out. It meant he'd had what he wanted and now he was getting ready for the day ahead. A day in which again she had no part.

All that had changed was this time, instead of making do with an embrace that left them both unsatisfied and on edge, Damon had enjoyed her body to the full. Several times.

She meant nothing to him but carnal pleasure. And of course, an added twist to his revenge on the Manolis family.

She satisfied his ego.

She'd spent years satisfying her husband's ego.

Yet Damon was infinitely more dangerous than Alkis. Damon got closer to her long-buried emotions. He'd stripped away the façade behind which she hid, the veneer of cool sophistication that concealed the needy, vulnerable woman.

It was just imagination, hormones, forbidden fantasies that made last night seem special. She couldn't let that cloud her determination to remain aloof and preserve herself from the devastation he'd inflict if she let him close.

She had to do what Damon did so well—separate sex and emotion. Compartmentalise her life and keep her feelings locked away. *He'd* never suffer romantic daydreams about her.

Callie marshalled her resolve. She would be strong. Damon would never realise how profoundly he'd affected her.

How for a short time he'd reawakened naïve, girlish dreams of happily-ever-after with a man who seemed perfect for her. Caring and patient when she was in pain. Tender yet powerful and outrageously seductive in bed.

Spinning threads of wonder and ecstasy that stopped her thinking straight.

Allowing her control. The right to choose. She blinked furiously. How precious that had seemed last night.

Yet there'd *been* no choice. She'd been utterly ensnared by his potent seduction. Unable to escape. And he knew it.

The man she'd fallen for was a fantasy. He was *not* Damon. She had to remember that.

Callie would go her own way as soon as she could. Carve

a future for herself. Despite her lack of qualifications or work experience, she'd find a job and save. No matter how many years it took she'd earn enough to start her business, achieve her dream. She'd live her own life.

It would be all right.

Why, then, did her eyes mist with hot, prickling tears as her hand slid over that empty pillow? Why did her lip wobble so she had to bite down hard to keep it still and stifle the wrenching sob of pain that rose in her aching throat?

This was what she'd feared. Not the physical intimacy, though she'd known moments of doubt last night as Damon led her down paths, to experiences that were completely new. It was the sense of being swamped, overwhelmed by a force stronger than herself, that threatened to steal her identity.

The force binding her to Damon was stronger than blackmail. Her craving for tenderness had become a shackle, tying her to a man who would never care for her.

Callie would resist it. She refused to be a victim any longer.

Damon whistled softly between his teeth as he towelled his hair. Even the cold shower, necessary to keep his libido in check long enough to get out the door to the office, hadn't doused his buoyant mood.

She was his. At last Callie was his. She was as delicious as he remembered.

More. She was…more.

He'd never felt so jubilant after a night with a lover.

His hands stilled as the thought flashed into his brain that Callie wasn't like his previous women.

He ignored the idea. It was simply the result of supreme sexual satisfaction. Sex had never been this good. Callie was more than anything he'd ever imagined.

It had been tempting to stay in bed, consigning his morning's meetings to oblivion.

Far too tempting.

Damon prided himself on his willpower. He hadn't got

where he was by getting sidetracked. He didn't intend to start now. Especially when, for all her sweet abandon, he knew remaining would be a measure of her power over him.

No woman had that sort of power.

He turned to drape the towel over a rail then froze as a thought lodged. He felt more pleasure, more excitement finally having Callie where he wanted her than at acquiring Manolis Enterprises. That had once loomed above him like an unreachable goal.

A woman, *this* woman, meant more than the goal that had sent him into business all those years ago.

Hair prickled his nape and a twist of something like apprehension coiled in his belly.

Impossible!

Swiftly he dressed, holding at bay the subversive snippets of thought that threatened to distract him.

How his lust for business success had faded this last year or two. Outstripped now by his lust for one woman.

No! He wasn't a one-woman man. Not yet. Not till the time came to settle down and start a family.

How Callie had been everything he'd expected, yet different. Unexpected. In some ways almost innocent.

Could it be? After years of marriage? After the way she'd come to him the first time: so easy and uninhibited?

No, it was a tactic she'd used to excite him. Her apparent surprise and inexperience in the shower just showed she could pander to a man's fantasies—playing the role of shy ingénue to complement her obvious sensuality.

Yet his hands slowed on his shirt buttons, remembering the look on her face as he'd knelt before her: trepidation mixed with excitement.

She'd acted like an inexperienced virgin.

He knew for a fact she was anything but that.

Deftly he tucked in his shirt and reached for a comb. The surge of heat in his groin, the warmth in his chest slowly dissipated.

Had she conned him again? Didn't she know he wanted her just as she was? The *real* her. Not some carefully constructed persona like the one she'd created at her uncle's behest.

He preferred she didn't play such masquerades. He was a straight-down-the-line sort of guy. That was what he expected from her. Honesty. Was that too much to ask?

'There's no need to pretend you're asleep.'

Damon's voice came from too close. Callie had hoped he'd leave her, apparently sleeping, when he departed. She needed time to pull herself together before she faced him.

Perhaps he wanted to gloat. Men enjoyed revelling in their triumphs.

For a fleeting time she'd thought perhaps with him it could be different.

Reluctantly she opened her eyes. He stood beside the bed, fully dressed, his hair sleek from the shower. He was tall, dark and utterly gorgeous.

Her throat closed on a convulsion of emotion and her chest ached as if too full. She wanted to stroke her finger down the proud, skewed line of his nose, taste the heat of his lips with hers, feel his hands on her body.

His next words remedied that desire.

'Every morning you pretend not to be awake when I leave. That stops now.'

Guilty heat shot through her, yet she said nothing.

'I refuse to be ignored. Especially in my own bed.' His lips curled in a satisfied smile. 'Especially after last night.'

Suddenly Damon looked like a particularly hungry, particularly dangerous cat. And Callie felt like a tiny cornered mouse. She shuffled back from the edge of the bed, sitting up and drawing the sheet over her naked breasts.

She should have dressed while she had the chance.

He stepped closer till he was up against the bed, looking down.

'A kiss would be an excellent way to say goodbye before I leave for the office.'

Yet his deep voice, his hooded gaze told her he was considering more than a kiss.

He wanted her again.

In the light of day that scared her more than ever. His passion sucked her under, obliterating every defence she had. It made her vulnerable.

'Is that part of the job description for mistresses?' Defiance was her only defence.

His head jerked back, his shoulders stiffening as his lips turned down in displeasure.

'After what we've shared, you would begrudge a kiss?' Anger underscored his suddenly cool tone.

'No.' Callie's defiance ebbed.

It was a losing battle, trying to resist Damon when her body clamoured for him. What she wanted was to melt in his embrace and let him seduce her away to that fantasy paradise they'd discovered together.

She looked around for a robe but there was nothing to cover her nakedness. Instead she tugged the sheet loose and pulled it round her as she rose to her knees.

Damon's palm was warm on her cheek, his breath sweet temptation against her lips as she stretched up towards him.

She wanted this as much as he. It did no good to pretend otherwise. Her heartbeat accelerated in anticipation.

'Better, much better,' he murmured. 'But there's no need for the display of false modesty.'

His other hand curled round the sheet at her breasts and yanked. Horrified, she grabbed the fine linen and sat back on her heels, securing the cloth tightly around her.

'What are you talking about?'

An expression she couldn't read flitted across his face. His mouth hardened.

'You needn't pretend to be so innocent. I don't need games like that to pique my interest.'

His eyes glittered, scorching a trail down to her empty belly and lower, where an insidious pulse of excitement started beating.

'I'm not playing a game,' she responded, bewildered. 'I don't know what you mean.'

Abruptly Damon sat on the bed and reached out to her, his hand cupping her chin so she couldn't evade him.

'You act like you've never let a man see you naked.'

'Is it a crime to feel modest about baring my body?' Indignation snaked through her.

'All I'm saying is you can drop the pretence. I know who I took on when I accepted you as my mistress.'

Despite the warmth of his hand against her skin a chill engulfed her. That sounded remarkably like an insult. As if he was magnanimous admitting her into his presence.

'You've lost me.' Her chin tilted higher.

He jerked his head up impatiently, his hand dropping away. Yet his gaze held her snared like a bird before the hypnotic eyes of a deadly predator.

'Last night you pretended you'd never had oral sex. That you were inexperienced in quite a few things.'

Despite the disapproval in his eyes, Callie didn't miss the flare of heat as he remembered what they'd done together in the bathroom and here, in his wide bed.

Embarrassment was a swirling wave engulfing her, making her skin glow.

She wanted to look away but hiding wasn't the answer.

'As it happens, I hadn't. Is that a crime?'

The shock on Damon's face would have been ludicrous if it weren't so insulting.

What did he think she was?

Then she remembered exactly what he thought of her—some unprincipled socialite whose time was spent shopping and having affairs.

The last of the sweet, piercing joy she'd discovered as Damon made love to her through the night splintered and vanished.

Good, she decided over the soundless keening of her bruised soul. It had been a mirage anyway. Better she face that fact now than spin hopeless dreams.

'I told you, there's no need to act the innocent.' His jaw jutted belligerently. 'If I want you to play games in bed I'll let you know. In the meantime, don't lie. I don't like it.'

'I'm not lying.' Her voice trembled with an indignation so fierce she strove to control her larynx. 'I did what you wanted, didn't I? That's enough.'

More than enough. The bliss she'd found in his bed was tarnished. She felt unclean.

'And I find your attitude insulting,' she added between clenched teeth. Bad enough when he'd misjudged her before. But now, after the intimacies of last night, the pain of his mistrust carved right through her.

She'd been right not to read too much into what had after all been just sex.

The trouble was the experience was still so overwhelming for her. She hadn't been able to shake the ridiculous idea that there'd been something special about the connection between them.

Damon was probably just as 'special' with all his lovers, she realised bitterly.

Yet she felt betrayed.

'*My* attitude?' He rose to his feet so swiftly she got dizzy. He towered over her, dominating the bed, but at least now he wasn't so close that he overwhelmed her. 'I think you need to consider your own first.'

'What, do I need to consult some *Mistress's Handbook of Etiquette*? I suppose I've broken an unwritten rule.' Callie found refuge in sarcasm, hoping to hide the raw hurt of his accusations.

'Don't tell me I didn't satisfy you,' she jibed before he could respond. 'That would be a lie. You were *well*-satisfied. Several times.'

Even if she *was* incompetent as a lover, his expertise had

more than made up for it. In her naïvety she'd assumed her eagerness had pleased him as it had that first time on the beach. Clearly she'd been wrong.

'What are you saying?' He crossed his arms over his chest. Even in a dark silk shirt and tailored trousers he looked dangerous, as if civilisation was the thinnest veneer to the untamed, primitive man beneath. 'That I seduced an innocent that day on the beach? Even after you'd been married for six years?' His expression of disbelief made her bristle. 'I don't believe in fairy stories, Callista.'

His tone, his attitude, the echo of her uncle's disapproving use of her full name: it was the final straw.

After years bottling up the truth and the pain of her disastrous marriage, it was too much. Raw fury, white-hot and overwhelming, rushed through her, obliterating all else.

Deliberately Callie turned and made a production of plumping up the pillows behind her. Then she leaned back, feeling his eyes on her but pretending not to notice.

'Don't worry,' she purred in the deadly saccharine tone that only true disgust could conjure. 'I didn't claim that I came to you a virgin. Someone else had that pleasure.'

She paused, remembering with a jolt just how little the gift of her innocence had meant to her first lover.

The first man to betray her.

A tremor of dark emotion ripped through her and she folded her hands tighter across her breasts, angling her chin in what she hoped was an unconcerned attitude.

'However, I'm not quite the tart you imagine. My sexual history isn't quite as…adventurous or as extensive as you seem to expect. I haven't had a lover in a long time.'

'Lover…husband, don't play semantics.' Damon's gravel tone indicated his displeasure.

'I mean…' she paused and turned to meet him eye to eye. By rights he should burst into flames and shrivel up before her, such was the concentrated dislike in her glare '…my husband was impotent. The marriage was never consummated.'

She let him absorb that for a moment.

His eyes widened and sparked with surprise.

'And,' she continued, with the perfect, cut-crystal diction of outraged virtue, 'I was faithful to my marriage vows. Unlike the women you apparently mix with, I never took a lover to my bed while I was married.'

The silence thundered with the rush of blood in her ears, with Damon's unspoken questions and the echo of her words.

'You ask me to believe all that?' His voice had a hoarse edge that told her she'd finally unsettled him. But she was beyond feeling triumph at such a petty victory.

'Frankly, Damon, I don't care what you believe. You accused me of lying, so I set the record straight.'

Let him think what he liked. She was beyond caring.

After years of her being pilloried as a gold digger, and by her suspicious husband as an adulteress, it was incredibly liberating to blurt out the truth.

A burden lifted from her shoulders, as if by sharing just that one aspect of her disastrous marriage she shed some of the cramping pain that had filled her for so long.

Maybe forging a new start would be easier than she'd imagined. Perhaps she just had to reach out and grasp what she wanted. She shifted her gaze to the new daylight edging the curtains.

The thought gave her courage.

'Since it seems I don't satisfy you, Damon, I think we should end our arrangement.' She darted a sideways glance, taking in lowering dark brows and his preternaturally still form. He looked as if he'd had the shock of his life.

'I've given you what you wanted,' she continued. 'I kept my part of the bargain.'

She pressed back against the pillows. Once she was away from here, once she'd escaped the coils of desire that ensnared her when Damon was near, she'd start anew.

'I'll leave today.'

* * *

Tousled blonde hair framed her face and flirted around her breasts and bare shoulders. Wrapped in a sheet, looking thoroughly bedded, she shouldn't wield the authority she did.

Yet she was breathtaking: far too sexy yet curiously austere. As superb as a warrior queen, issuing a royal decree.

His libido leapt into overdrive. He'd never before come across a woman who had that delicious combination of decisive, demanding female with a take-no-prisoners attitude and warm, seductive lover.

There was a power about her, a potent vitality that had been missing earlier. Even at her most haughty, sparring verbally with him over the past few weeks, she hadn't been this mesmerising.

Guilt engulfed him. Was she telling the truth? Instinct said she was. That he'd ruthlessly pursued a woman who, though not innocent, was far from the sexually experienced partner he'd assumed.

That didn't negate her manipulative plot with her uncle or her mercenary first marriage. Though if she'd spent her married life without her husband in her bed that perhaps explained her breathtaking enthusiasm for sexual pleasure.

But it altered the situation enormously.

Had Damon demanded too much? Too fast? He'd been insatiable and had given free rein to long-thwarted desire.

Yet despite her occasional hesitance, she'd been willing. So willing just the thought of her in bed threatened to blow the lid off his control.

More, the knowledge that what they'd shared was somehow right…more right than anything he'd had with any woman, overcame his pangs of conscience.

He couldn't let her go. Not yet.

'You're not going anywhere.' His voice was thick with the desire that filled every pore, strained every sinew.

She swung her head round, staring at him with the eyes of a seductress, a sorceress. Surely she'd bewitched him. Desire consumed him, obliterating all else.

No evidence now of any vulnerability in her. Not the innocent nor the anguished woman he'd held in his arms aboard the *Circe*. The woman who'd evoked all his protective instincts.

The memory of her last night, the sight of her now, proud and defiant and alluring, ripped the oxygen from his lungs.

'I beg your pardon?'

Damon's lips quirked in appreciation. She really did have attitude. So superior. So irresistible.

'I said you're not leaving.'

Even the moue of surprise on her soft pink lips tugged at his control. Had she really thought she'd leave after one night in his bed?

She was either incredibly naïve or playing some deep Machiavellian game.

He spun on his foot and paced the room, facing his doubts and his conscience.

'That's not for you to decide.'

He turned back to find her sitting taut and straight, her chin notched haughtily, her eyes blazing.

His belly tightened and some alien sensation stirred deep in his chest.

He *couldn't* let her go.

'Isn't it?' He paused, waiting as she digested his purposeful tone.

'But I delivered on my end of the bargain!' She leaned forward, eager to press her point.

His eyes dropped to the hint of cleavage visible as the fisted hand securing the sheet moved. With a supreme effort he returned his gaze to her face.

'You were to be my mistress for as long as I want.' He walked towards the bed, tugging at the tie that suddenly seemed too tight around his neck. 'And I still want. One night is barely a deposit. We'll discuss your plan to leave in a few months.'

Why this unholy pleasure in baiting her? The fire in her

eyes ignited a flame of expectation that swamped the last of his scruples.

No other woman, ever, had affected him like this.

She froze, her mouth working as if lost for words.

'Too bad.' Her eyes narrowed and she pressed back against the bed head. 'One night was more than enough for me.'

Through the taut silence her eyes held his defiantly. Finally her lashes dropped and her gaze skated to the windows on the other side of the room.

Not so poised and certain, then.

'I don't want you,' she said in a voice that was too high, too light. Telling this lie didn't come easily. 'I never wanted you. And your ego won't allow you to force an unwilling woman to stay in your bed.' That note of triumph only stirred his fighting spirit.

'Liar,' he whispered as he dropped his tie. Of course she wanted him. Her eyes widened as she followed the movement. 'You don't convince me, Callie. You won't leave.'

'Why shouldn't I?' Her expression turned arctic. 'Are you threatening to chase after my cousin again? You're big on threats, aren't you?'

Damon shook his head. He had no desire to become Aristides Manolis' son-in-law.

'No threat required, princess. This isn't about Angela. This is about you and me.'

A smile hovered on his lips as he approached.

She swallowed hard, her eyes on him as he paced to the base of the bed.

'You want me. You want to stay here, with me.' His gesture encompassed the vast, rumpled bed. With his other hand he flicked open the top button of his shirt. And the next. And the next.

Somewhere down the row her mouth opened a fraction and her eyes darkened to a deep emerald glow.

Damon shucked off his shoes and stripped off his socks.

When he straightened she'd moved further away, hands clenching the sheet to her collarbone.

'What are you doing?' Definitely a wobble in that voice now. She held herself like a monarch, oblivious to the actions of commoners like him. But her eyes gave her away.

Ah, Callie. Why fight it? Why not admit that, for now at least, he was the man who fired her blood and ignited her senses? The man who could give her everything she desired.

Excitement surged as he remembered her claim that he'd been the only man in six years. The thought thrilled his masculine ego.

As if she'd kept herself just for him.

Madness. She'd done no such thing. But that didn't stifle his pleasure.

'What am I doing? Proving you wrong, lover.'

He shrugged out of his shirt, noting the way her gaze followed the movement.

Not so aloof now, princess.

His belt slid to the floor as he climbed onto the bed. Slowly he prowled its length on hands and knees. Callie's eyes rounded as she shrank back.

His knees straddled her feet, her legs, her thighs. Still she glared back, a study in aristocratic disdain. But he had her measure now. He knew that behind the façade pulsed a heart as hungry for passion as his own.

The knowledge was immeasurably exciting.

Callie was exciting.

His heart drummed a staccato beat as he felt her warmth beneath him. He breathed deep, inhaling the fragrance of sweet female skin and the sultry scent of sex.

'You won't change my mind.' She blurted the words out, but they were a poor camouflage. Her nipples peaked like succulent fresh berries beneath the sheet. Her chest rose and fell with her rapid breathing.

'You want me, don't you, Callie?'

She shook her head, her lips a flat line.

He contemplated a frontal assault, kissing her till she capitulated. But that wasn't enough. He wanted the words. He needed to know her hunger matched his.

Braced above her but not touching, he lowered his head and pressed an open-mouthed kiss on the pleasure point where her neck met her shoulder.

She jerked beneath him.

Damon grazed his teeth across the spot and was rewarded with a judder of response. He watched her skin prickle and repeated the caress. The rhythm of her breathing altered, its tempo rattling out of control.

'Say it, lover. Say you need me.'

Callie sidled away. He prevented her simply by sliding his hand under the linen to cup her warm, full breast.

A bolt of energy sheared straight to his groin. He wondered if he had the control to manage a slow, persuasive seduction when every hormone screamed the need for haste.

Callie turned him into a man he barely recognised.

Her breath sawed as he kissed along her shoulder and back to her neck.

'Say it, Callie. Or walk out the door.'

He moved his hand, tracing his fingertip in spiralling circles towards her nipple.

She gasped as he tugged the sensitive point.

The sound of her, the feel and scent and memory of her stiffened his body to breaking point. Just like that.

What had been intended as erotic torment for her was torture for him too.

'I—'

'Yes, Callie?' He pressed another kiss to her collarbone then across her rapidly working throat.

'I...need you, Damon.' Her voice was deliciously hoarse.

His heart stuttered as slim, delicate fingers caressed his shoulders, slid down his chest, exploring across, up and then inexorably down.

Relief shuddered through him.

Damon slanted his mouth hungrily over hers, sinking into her generous depths like a sailor coming home to port after a long and dangerous odyssey.

He'd expected triumph when she capitulated. But the surge of warmth and overwhelming tenderness that enveloped him at her welcome was new.

For an instant it teased his mind. Then, inevitably, he fell into the pleasurable oblivion of Callie's loving.

CHAPTER ELEVEN

'THANKS for your hospitality, Damon. It's been a profitable meeting. And a delight getting to know you, Callie. I'll enjoy returning the favour when you visit.'

Callie smiled. 'It was lovely meeting you too, Paulo.' She watched the older man shake hands with Damon, surprised to discover how much she liked Damon's associates and friends.

This business lunch at Athens' picturesque Mikrolimano Harbour had revealed Damon as a relaxed and attentive host, as well as an astute entrepreneur.

There'd been wealthy businessmen and their partners, most now leaving the marina for the fleet of limos that would take them to their destinations. None had been in a hurry to go. All valued Damon's opinion and friendship.

'My pleasure,' Damon responded with an easy smile. 'We'll look forward to taking you up on your offer.'

They were going to Brazil? Callie shot a startled glance at Damon.

He sent her an unreadable look. 'I need to fit in a visit to South America in the next few months.'

Callie digested that. They'd been together several weeks. Callie still reeled at the intensity of their relationship. Surrendering to Damon hadn't been the punishment she expected. It had been mutual pleasure. No winner, no loser. Just the pair of them caught in a conflagration of desire.

Callie was alternately scared and delighted by the passionate woman his loving had revealed. But she'd assumed a passion that flared so brightly would burn itself out in time. Wasn't that why Damon never stayed with any one woman? Because eventually he tired of her?

But he was talking about months into the future.

Could she survive months with him and emerge unscathed? Already she found herself wishing for more. Wishing to understand the complex man who delighted her in bed, but remained an enigma outside of it.

'And you'll bring Callie? Excellent.' Callie turned to find Mariana, Paulo's gorgeous, dark-haired wife beaming at her. 'That will give me a chance to show you some of the places I told you about.'

Her smile was genuine and Callie responded automatically. She was still surprised at the warmth with which she'd been greeted by Mariana and the other women today. In her experience beautiful women with wealthy partners were more likely to be suspicious of potential rivals.

'That means shopping,' Paulo groaned theatrically. 'She'll ruin me yet.'

Mariana turned and gave him a playful punch in the arm then kissed his cheek.

Callie was dumbfounded at the pang of envy she felt as she watched the older couple. Her experience of marriage had put her off the institution. Especially as so many of her late husband's friends were in unhappy relationships: mismatched couples brought together by greed, duty or convenience.

For years she'd dreamed only of freedom and independence. But watching Mariana and Paulo...

'You'll enjoy yourself, Callie.' Damon's deep voice interrupted her thoughts. 'Paulo's home is the last word in luxury. And we'll visit my resorts. Sybaritic pleasure guaranteed.'

He thought that was what she wanted? She opened her mouth to disabuse him, but the words crumbled on her tongue as he reached out. One finger stroked a wisp of hair behind her ear then slipped down her cheek, under her jaw line, to nudge her chin up. Suddenly he was only a kiss away.

His eyes blazed with an intensity that had been missing moments before.

The fine hairs on her arms rose and a tingling started deep in her belly as she remembered his lips moving against hers. The swirl of fire as his tongue found hers and desire spiralled out of control.

'Come, Paulo. It's time we left.'

Startled, Callie dragged her gaze from Damon's and turned. Embarrassment warmed her cheeks as she met Mariana's understanding smile and heard Paulo chuckle.

'Very well, woman. We have matters of our own to see to, eh?' He waggled his eyebrows so obviously Callie had to stifle a smile.

He shepherded his wife to the door of the luxury cruiser's main cabin. 'By the way, Damon, do you still have that dog?' There was a sparkle in Paulo's eyes.

'What would I do with a dog? I travel too much.'

'She didn't die after all?' Mariana sounded upset.

'Of course not.' Paulo looped his arm around her. 'She wouldn't dare. Not after Damon took her under his wing.'

Intrigued, Callie looked from one to the other. 'What dog?'

'Just a pup,' Damon said brusquely. 'It was injured in a car accident.'

'The poor thing was being trained as a guide dog,' Mariana added, 'when a speeding car hit her. We were the next car along and Damon stopped to help.'

'Which meant hours finding a good vet and sorting things out with its owners,' Paulo added.

'Sorting things out?'

'They wanted to put her down,' Damon said gruffly. 'Just because she had a leg amputated. I arranged to take her.'

'Buy her, don't you mean? And pay the vet bills.'

'Easy to do, Paulo. I'm not exactly short of cash.' Damon looked as if he wanted to change the subject.

Mariana leaned forward and gave him a motherly pat on the cheek. 'You did more, Damon. You took the poor animal home yourself.' She turned to Callie. 'And when he found how long the waiting list was for trained companion dogs he endowed a new breeding facility and training program.'

Fascinated, Callie watched Damon's cheeks darken. He looked embarrassed.

'One of your projects to set the world straight,' Paulo murmured. 'You're always trying to make things right.' He looked at Callie. 'You'll find it's a fixation of Damon's.'

'You exaggerate as usual, Paulo. You'd have done the same if I hadn't.'

'So what did happen to the mutt?'

Damon shrugged. 'My nephew took a fancy to her and she bonded with him.' He rubbed his chin, his expression rueful. 'Only he insists on bringing her sailing. Keeping a four-year-old and his three-legged dog from sliding off a slippery deck has its challenges.'

Paulo barked with laughter and clapped a hand on Damon's shoulder. 'I knew you hadn't got rid of it. I just wish you were this soft in our business negotiations.'

'So you could fleece me? I'd like to see the day.'

After more farewells Callie watched Damon escort their guests ashore.

He was passionate, single-minded and ruthless in getting what he wanted. Yet Damon had an unexpected tender streak. He'd comforted her aboard *Circe*. He'd organised a chopper to take them to his home, understanding her fear of sailing.

What sort of self-absorbed tycoon cosseted the woman he'd blackmailed into his bed? Adopted a maimed pup? Went out of his way to fund a guide-dog centre?

She didn't understand him. She'd thought him cruel, relentless, motivated only by a desire for revenge and a taste for sensual pleasure. But there was more to his character.

Donating to charity didn't make him a saint. Alkis had

supported charities, but on the advice of accountants, only to minimise tax. Never because he was moved by their cause.

She watched Damon walk back aboard and felt an overwhelming need to understand him. To know where she fitted in his world.

'What did Paulo mean about you trying to set the world to rights?'

He paused then sauntered across the room.

'Paulo exaggerates.' He met her enquiring gaze and she knew he wasn't going to elaborate. Instead the look in his eyes was intent, making her feel suddenly too warm, too vulnerable.

She hurried into speech. 'You were pleased with today's lunch? With your meeting?'

In her experience men were easily distracted by what interested them most—their plans to increase profits and prestige. If today's lunch was any indicator, Damon had reason to smile.

He shrugged and she couldn't help but follow the movement of his rangy shoulders.

'The discussions went well. It made a pleasant change to meet on board rather than in an office. Plus there was a lot of interest in this latest cruiser design.'

His nod encompassed the vast cabin with its aura of wealth. From the impossibly plush carpet to the exquisite marquetry woodwork, sleek, modern design and equipment, the room was the perfect setting for a billionaire.

Yet Callie remembered how Damon had looked, his hair rumpled by a sea breeze, his feet bare on the decking of *Circe*. As if he belonged. As if he enjoyed the unfettered freedom and simplicity of the grand old yacht.

Part of her hankered to experience that moment again. She'd felt for a short, incredible time that, with Damon's support, she might even conquer her fear of sailing.

'How about you, Callie? Did you enjoy yourself?' His question took her by surprise. He sounded genuinely curious.

'It was fun. They're nice people.' She'd enjoyed herself more than at any social engagement during her marriage.

What was different? The people? Damon's friends had none of the brash self-importance of Alkis' cronies. And the man at her side? With Alkis she'd always felt restricted, judged, undercut by his disapproval. With Damon...

'You were a hit today,' he murmured, his expression intimate. 'The men in particular were impressed and very jealous of me.' His smile was all male triumph.

Her mouth primmed as a cold, all too familiar weight dropped in her chest.

So that was why he'd invited her. She should have known.

He'd invited her to be his hostess, to entertain the women while the men discussed business then help him look after their guests over lunch. She'd felt a spurt of pleasure that Damon valued her assistance. He must have some respect for her, even if only for her social skills.

How pathetic to cling to such a crumb!

The gleam in his eyes told its own story. Things weren't so simple. She remembered the quickly veiled interest in several pairs of masculine eyes today, and the way the single men went out of their way to engage her attention.

Damon had been playing a game of one-upmanship, displaying his latest acquisition. His mistress.

The metallic tang of disappointment filled her mouth.

She should have guessed. To him she was a possession. For a while, enjoying a discussion with the women about house design and furnishings, she'd almost forgotten.

Damon didn't want her for her mind or personality. It was her body—the way it looked and how it could satisfy his needs—that counted.

'I think Rafael would have tried to steal you away if given half a chance.'

Damon's eyes bored into her, waiting for her reaction. What did he expect? Pleasure? Excitement?

He moved in a world where rich men acquired and dropped beautiful lovers on a whim. Where women prowled for wealthy protectors and men held ultimate power.

Her stomach churned. She'd had a taste of independence when Alkis died but now she was caught again in that net of male domination.

'You were the most beautiful woman here.'

Callie raised her eyebrows.

She had no illusions about her appearance. Her eyes were nice but her mouth was too wide and her nose too long. Only good posture prevented her looking gangly, despite her curves. Most of her allure was artificial—clothes, attitude, bearing. Her eye for colour and design helped her create an illusion of beauty.

For six years she'd been a possession displayed to prop up her husband's ego and even, she'd discovered later, to lure potential targets for his commercial plans.

She'd been paraded, slavered over and treated like a brainless mannequin. The memories were bitter and raw.

The last thing she needed was compliments on her looks.

She spun on her heel, pacing to the sideboard and the champagne flute she'd barely touched. Swiftly she tilted the crystal to her mouth and swallowed. Effervescent bubbles cascaded over her lips and burst on her tongue. They obliterated the taste of disappointment, though they couldn't quench her simmering resentment.

A few months of freedom and she'd foolishly allowed herself to forget her place in a rich man's world.

'Are we celebrating?' Damon's warm velvet voice caressed her bare neck. A shiver rippled across her skin as she registered the invitation in his tone. He stood so close his heat encompassed her. His musky salt scent invaded her space.

His lips brushed her nape once, twice and she melted. Despite her fury she trembled at his caress.

The flute landed on the wood with a click.

'No. I was just thirsty.'

A hand on her arm made her turn.

She found herself skewered by a dark, unrelenting gaze that sliced to the core of her.

'What's wrong, Callie?'

'I may be your mistress, but I don't like being made to feel cheap.'

'Cheap?' His eyes narrowed and he stepped close, filling her personal space with his big body, his spicy scent, his vibrating anger. 'Someone insulted you? Who was it?'

Callie shook her head, taken aback by his sudden wrath. He looked positively dangerous.

'No one.' She backed a fraction to find herself jammed up against the sideboard. 'I meant the way you invited me here just to show me off as your latest plaything.'

Damon's eyes sparked fire but his words were soft. 'You think that's why I invited you?'

'Why else? Up till now my place has been in your bed. Now you're busy gloating over how jealous your friends are.'

'You read all this from my comment about them admiring you?' He frowned.

She lifted her shoulders in a tight shrug. 'It's how men are.'

'Not this man.' It was a muted growl that made the hairs on her arms prickle. 'I don't need the jealousy of others to prop up my ego.' He thrust his face forward till his banked fury enveloped her. 'You're confusing me with someone else.' There was no mistaking his sincerity, or that he felt insulted. 'Your husband perhaps?'

Callie looked away. The memory of Alkis and his controlling ways was still too strong.

'I don't discuss my marriage.' Pushing that hurt aside was the only way she'd kept going.

'Yet you judge me because of his behaviour. Is that it?'

Callie kept her gaze fixed on the view of the harbour, intimidated by his righteous indignation.

'Didn't it occur to you that I invited you because I wanted you with me? Because I like having you beside me?'

Startled, Callie froze.

'Because I thought my guests would enjoy your company, which they did. And because I thought you'd enjoy theirs.'

Slowly she turned her face up to his.

He looked angry. Impatient. Sincere.

'You look for insults where there are none.'

'I'm sorry,' she murmured, thrown by his intensity, feeling guilty and foolish at her suspicions. 'I enjoyed today. Thank you. Especially meeting Paulo and Mariana. They have such a strong relationship.'

He tilted his head to one side. 'You sound surprised.'

Callie's lips twisted ruefully. 'Happy marriages are a rare commodity.'

'Including yours?'

She sighed. He just didn't give up. 'Including mine.' Callie sidestepped, gaining precious space. She didn't want to talk about Alkis. 'It's nice to see a couple so devoted.'

'My parents were like that.' Damon surprised her with the personal observation. 'And my siblings are all happily shackled.'

'You sound very close.' Maybe if she'd had a sister or brother she'd still have that sort of special bond with someone who loved her.

Damon stepped nearer. 'My sisters say too close. That I'm overprotective, that before they married I always tried to arrange their lives.'

'Whereas now you have to divert your energies into saving stray dogs?' Or settling an old score with the family who'd wronged his. Was that what Paulo had meant about him ensuring things turned out right?

'Not *all* my energies.' His voice was a silken skein of suggestion as he stroked her cheek, brow and lips.

Instantly Callie's eyelids lowered and she swayed close, drawn by the desire that pulsed between them. Each time it was the same—something she couldn't fight. A hunger that fed on itself, growing stronger by the day.

'I should go.' Her voice was husky. 'I have an appointment in the city.' She needed to prove to herself that she retained some shred of self-control.

His hand stilled. 'An appointment?'

'With my lawyer. I'd prefer not to be late.'

'Ah, I thought you'd dressed conservatively.' He gestured to her honey-beige suit, aquamarine camisole and high heels. 'But I like it.' His smile sent her pulse racing. His hand dropped to her lapel, sliding along the fabric.

'Is there some legal problem?' His question surprised her. She shrugged, half her attention on his wandering hand.

Today's meeting was to discuss her non-existent trust fund. She'd heard nothing from her uncle about her inheritance and her calls to Angela had centred on Aunt Desma. At least in that respect there was good news. The doctors had hopes she'd respond well to medication.

'Nothing I can't handle.'

Impenetrable eyes surveyed her so thoroughly she felt as if he stripped bare all her secrets.

'When is the appointment?' The liquid heat in his eyes told her he had plans for the afternoon that didn't include meeting with lawyers.

'In less than an hour.'

Damon's hand dropped, feathering past her breast in a stealthy caress that caught her breath. He stepped back.

'All right, then. Let's go. I'll drop you.'

His withdrawal stunned her. She'd expected him to ignore her plans and seduce her. Here. Now.

Disappointment fizzed.

He extended an arm and waited till she reluctantly tucked her arm in his.

For one instant she experienced a mad urge to lean against his solid bulk and blurt out her problems, as she had that day on his yacht.

Then logic kicked in, a savage blow to the solar plexus that sucked the air from her lungs.

Damon Savakis *was* her problem.

Damon strode quickly to the bedroom.

'Callie?' Still that fillip of excitement got him whenever he came home.

'Callie?' He entered the master suite and paused, disappointment crashing into him when he found it empty. She wasn't as he'd fantasised, in the sunken tub, waiting for him.

Since they'd moved to his Athens apartment she spent most days out on business of her own. She wasn't exactly secretive but she didn't offer information and after the little he'd gleaned about her marriage he didn't push. She was opening up to him only slowly.

He knew her spark of extra animation coincided with her trust fund becoming available.

He smiled. It was good to see the way she'd blossomed. She'd been gorgeous before, but now, with this inner glow of excitement, she was irresistible.

Damon headed down the hall. Maybe she was in the room she'd converted into an office. He knocked. Silence. He hesitated. He'd never entered the private space where her belongings were stored.

Finally he turned the handle. It wouldn't be the first time she hadn't heard him because she was listening to earphones. There was that memorable time in his private gym. She'd been working out in tight shorts and a skimpy top, oblivious to his arrival, and he'd…

Damon stopped as the door swung open.

He had a hazy memory of the room as it been, designer-styled cream chic.

The memory vanished as vibrant colours caught his eye, lush, rich and inviting. He frowned, *feeling* a difference in the atmosphere.

Stepping into Callie's room was like stepping into another world. One alive with her presence.

The pristine monochromatic style of his modern apartment suddenly seemed soulless as he gazed around this space.

The bed was pushed into the corner to make space for a massive draughtsman's desk. The cream coverlet was piled with cushions in purples, greens and blues that made him think how much he wanted to make love to her here.

More cushions beckoned on a low sofa. On a glass coffee-table was an arrangement of lilies, their scent reminding him of Callie's skin as they made love, sweet and musky.

On the walls were a series of...he didn't know the word. Hangings? Embroideries? Massive artworks of fabric and beads in the colours of the sea. They depicted the ocean in moods ranging from pearly calm to steely grey and dangerous, all finished with exquisite stitching.

He stepped close, drawn to one that depicted a pine-fringed beach with water the colour of Callie's eyes. He could almost reach out and touch the sea.

A squiggle of gold in one corner caught his eye. C.M.

Callie's work? Could it be?

He moved back, stunned. Callie had done this? He went from one piece to another. On each were the same initials.

Callie said she sewed. But she'd been so reticent he assumed she made little doilies like those his mother sewed.

Astounded, he pivoted. These belonged in a gallery.

Why did she hide her talent like this?

Curiosity got the better of him and he moved to the vast desk, taking in catalogues, business cards of artisans who worked in glass and wood and timber. Swatches of fabrics. And beside them a much thumbed folder. A business plan.

Damon was so engrossed he didn't feel a qualm about sitting down and leafing through the document.

Half an hour later he flexed his shoulders and leaned back in the chair, closing the last page.

What a mystery his lover was.

She had outstanding talent. Even he, a philistine when it came to the decorative arts, recognised her genius for creating mood and sensation through her fabric scenes.

Her business plan for an upmarket home-furnishings boutique was careful and well thought out. She'd made a few potential mistakes, but had done a professional job.

Where had she learned about starting a business? Her husband? Unlikely. Yet she'd acquired the skills she needed.

She was some woman.

Pride warmed him at her determination to start her enterprise. It reminded him of his own drive to learn and succeed in business.

He glanced round the room, bright and welcoming and warmly sensuous. Like Callie.

He reached out and brushed his hand across a padded box upholstered in silk, with a beaded flying fish leaping across the top. Instinctively he knew Callie had made it. His hands curled around its soft edges, its glittering decoration.

Sitting in her space, Damon felt the warmth, the vibrancy, the secret something that drew him to Callie as to no other woman.

She'd turned his ideas about women on their heads.

Like the day at Mikrolimano when she'd entertained his guests. He'd known she'd be the perfect hostess. He hadn't hesitated in asking her, though he'd never invited any previous mistress to do so.

Nevertheless he'd been curious about her response to so much male interest. She'd been friendly but not too friendly. She'd spent most of her time laughing with the women and seemed almost oblivious of the stir she caused till later when she'd snapped at him.

Because she thought him like her husband? Something about her marriage was at the heart of her reserve.

For Callie wasn't the woman he'd first thought.

Prickly, independent, intelligent, fabulously responsive. She never pandered to his ego. She'd stood up to him time and again. She continually refused his gifts. She engaged his mind as well as his libido.

Callie was anything but a calculating man-eater.

She turned him inside out. For the first time he was no longer focused solely on the next merger, the next business triumph.

He wanted more. More of Callie.

CHAPTER TWELVE

'You mustn't let business take up all your time, Damon! Say you'll come to Kefalonia.'

The woman's gilded nails wrapped around Damon's sleeve and tugged him into contact with her over-abundant, unnaturally firm breast. It was as enticing as cuddling up to an overblown beach ball.

She turned scarlet lips up and her extravagant perfume closed like a fog around him.

'It will be a very select house party, Damonaki,' she purred, leaning still closer, as if her spouse wasn't just on the other side of the crowded theatre foyer. 'My husband won't be there till the weekend but I'll devote myself to entertaining you. Privately,' she added suggestively.

Her talons gripped tighter and he read the acquisitive glitter in her eyes.

Revulsion rose.

A swift glance at the throng around them made him swallow the curt retort hovering on his lips.

'I won't be available next week. Besides, my companion—'

'Callista Manolis?' He noted the barely restrained jealousy in the bottle-blonde's tone. 'She doesn't run your life. Not a strong, decisive man like you.' Her knee edged up his thigh. Bile filled his throat.

'Or,' she tilted her head speculatively, her mouth slackening in an expression of breathless excitement he found abhorrent, 'if you bring her we could have some fun. The three of us together.'

'I'm afraid that won't be possible.' The cool, cut-crystal tone interrupted before he could give voice to a pungent, earthy response.

He slid his arm free and turned towards the newcomer.

'Callie,' he murmured appreciatively. The sight of her, elegant and sexy in a high-necked, bare-shouldered black dress, was like a sip of pure spring water after swallowing something toxic.

Damon reached out and she slipped her hand into his. Warm, supple, it fitted perfectly. He was growing accustomed to this sense of rightness, having her with him.

'Damon and I have plans for that week,' Callie said, looking down from her superior height.

'You don't know which week we were discussing,' the other woman said. Her stiff facial muscles tightened more as she stared up at Callie.

Callie favoured Damon with a brief, knowing smile that made his heart drum faster. Even here, now, at this premiere event, he responded to the promise in her gold-flecked gaze.

'All Damon's weeks are booked up,' Callie asserted. 'Aren't they, Damon?'

Surprise transfixed him as that sultry, bedroom voice emerged from Callie's pink-glossed lips.

The only time he heard that tone was when they were alone and he'd driven her to the extremity of pleasure. Instinctively his body tightened.

'If you say so, *glikia mou.*'

He enjoyed the novelty of her playing the vamp. Usually she was reserved at events like this. As if the company of A-list celebrities and their cronies wasn't her style.

He leaned close and inhaled her fresh scent. It reminded him of sunny days and long, languorous loving.

Was she jealous? Was that why she'd appeared at his side?

The idea pleased him immensely. Though he had her in his

bed every night and the passion between them was a palpable force, part of her remained steadfastly closed to him.

He chose lovers who understood he wanted no emotional entanglements. But with Callie he found himself wanting more than physical gratification. The realisation unsettled him and he shoved it aside.

'Well,' huffed the other woman. 'Far be it from me to come between a happy couple.' Her eyes flashed. 'But don't forget, Damonaki,' she pressed close again, her mouth a wet pout, 'you're welcome any time. You'd find my hospitality memorable.'

She turned and undulated her way through the crowd.

Instantly Callie's hand tugged, as if to be released. He firmed his grip. Anger simmered in her green stare.

'Nice friends you have, *Damonaki*.' She didn't conceal her disgust, almost spitting out the ridiculous pet name. Yet she stood straight and proud, as if unfazed by that gross little scene.

'Jealous, lover?' Her lips flattened and he relented. 'The rescue wasn't necessary but thanks. One day her poor sot of a husband will find her propositioning someone and there'll be hell to pay.'

'He doesn't know?'

Damon shrugged. 'Probably. But if it's under his nose he'll have to do something about it and break a lifetime's habit of ignoring what he doesn't want to see.'

Was it any wonder he despised so many of society's 'best' people?

'Are you ready to go?' Looking at her in that dress made him want to strip her out of it. It was time they were alone.

'Don't you want to stay?'

Damon's lips firmed. For all Callie's abandon in his bed, his shower, on his sofa or even, on one memorable occasion, on his vast dining table, it was he who initiated intimacy. She still maintained that air of aloofness.

It tried his patience, even as it turned him on.

He released her hand, his fingers sliding over her wrist to

the sensitive pleasure point at her inner elbow. She shivered, her nipples peaking through the silky fabric as he caressed her.

'Let's go home.'

Home. Damon's huge penthouse *had* become home. More than Alkis' soulless mansion had been.

That was what had changed, Callie realised as Damon ushered her out to the waiting limo, his arm protective around her.

The deep freeze at her very core had begun to thaw.

Damon had done that. He mightn't trust her fully, might view her as a source of convenient sex, but he was more generous than any man she'd ever met. Generous with his time and himself, in ways that, to a woman used to being dismissed as an ornament, made something warm and soft burgeon inside.

Her weakness for him terrified her but she couldn't break away. Hadn't been able to since the morning he'd challenged her to walk out on him.

Callie was hooked on the passion blazing between them. It made her feel bliss.

More, it made her feel she was no longer alone against the world.

Damon wasn't generous as her husband had been, with easy gifts that proclaimed his ownership. Callie had made sure of it, refusing his offer of a designer dress, a glittery trinket from an exclusive jewellery house.

She would live within her means.

The recent, wonderful news that her trust fund had been restored fed her determination not to depend on a man's money again. More, she'd prove to herself she was capable, that she amounted to more than a woman whose sole accomplishment was as a man's trophy. She was hard at work on her plans, investigating commercial locations and sourcing products.

The suddenness of her lawyer's news still stunned her. She could barely believe her uncle had restored what he'd stolen. Had her lawyer pressured him somehow?

Her relationship with Greece's most eligible tycoon was

based on sex, not profit. It still shocked her that she wanted him so badly, so constantly, but she found a curious dignity in their arrangement. An equality.

Both were victims of an attraction they couldn't resist.

Damon had been piqued and curious when she didn't live up to her reputation of grasping money-grabber. His first gift, an oyster silk negligée that shouted 'mistress' with every stitch, had resurrected her fury at being manipulated into his bed.

That argument had ended with the silk in shreds and Damon smiling with feral pleasure as for the first time she took a dominant role in lovemaking. He'd looked up at her, moving above him as the world spun in kaleidoscope colours, and huskily threatened to buy her lingerie every day.

Callie's lips twitched at the memory.

Even her pride couldn't force her to relinquish this passionate relationship. Especially since she enjoyed being with Damon. He made her feel good about herself. Amazing when he'd originally forced their relationship and she'd wanted to hate him!

'What are you smiling about?' Damon tugged her close on the limo's back seat, his arm around her shoulders, his fingers a warm imprint on her bare flesh.

Desire ignited. It erupted, a tangible force, shooting darts of heat to her breasts and womb.

She put her hand on his muscled thigh and felt a judder of reaction as Damon's muscles tensed.

In this they were equals. Her smile widened.

'Nothing important. Tell me,' she turned to look him in the eye, 'who was that woman? Not an old flame?'

She was too old for Damon with her surgically enhanced face. She was vulgar. She was wrong for him in so many ways.

'You've got to be kidding.' His mouth twisted. He lifted her hand to his mouth, licking across her palm and up her wrist, creating an earth tremor of rapture.

Callie's mouth slackened and her pulse accelerated. She

leaned nearer, grateful for the privacy screen between them and Damon's driver.

'I didn't think your taste ran to anything so obvious.'

Damon cradled her hand to his face. Her heart kicked as his tongue swirled at the centre of her palm. Hot wires of tension snagged tight inside and her eyes fluttered closed.

'And you know all about my taste in women.'

Callie's eyes popped open to meet his impenetrable stare. She couldn't tell if he was serious or sarcastic.

Too late she realised she'd left herself open to a hurtful retort. Hadn't he accused her once of being obvious in her efforts to attract him?

Her fragile sense of well-being cracked.

'You intrigue me,' he murmured. 'Once I would have lumped you in the same group as her, with the morals of an alley cat.'

Callie stiffened and jerked her hand away, but he recaptured it easily, holding it between both of his.

'She's always on the prowl for fresh meat, a new lover she can corrupt with her tawdry charms.'

Numbly Callie shook her head, waiting for him to make a cutting remark about her own character. She should be inured to jibes. Hadn't she parried them endlessly before?

Yet after the intimacies of these recent weeks, the idea of such ravaging scorn cut her to the quick.

'They sicken me, the rich bitches who get what they want, no matter the cost to others.'

Damon wasn't looking at her. He stared at the streets of Athens, still crowded at this hour. Callie sensed it wasn't the city he saw. His thumb rubbed absently over her knuckles.

Curiosity stirred.

'She's not discreet,' she ventured. But the stares and wordless invitations directed at Damon by other women were often blatant.

No wonder he was so arrogantly certain of his attractiveness. He could have his pick. And every flashing-eyed stare made Callie's hackles rise.

He was hers.

She wasn't sharing.

Callie blinked, stunned at her vehement possessiveness.

'Discreet?' His snort of disgust brought her abruptly back to the present. 'Why be discreet when you can use wealth to smooth out any…inconveniences?'

'Damon?' His harsh expression scared her. He looked so angry. 'What is it?' Her fingers wrapped round his, tugging till he looked at her.

'Nothing,' he said at last. 'She reminded me of someone, that's all.'

Dark eyes held hers with an intensity that stilled her to immobility. He tilted her chin so he could see her face. She trembled under his intense scrutiny.

'What is it?' she whispered.

'We're almost home.' His voice held a sultry promise of pleasure and something more. 'Then we can talk.'

Since when had talking been the main item on Damon's agenda?

Twenty minutes later Callie sat alone on the shadowy rooftop terrace with its multimillion-dollar view across the city to the coast. The sweet scents of exotic flowers wafted from the exquisite penthouse garden.

She held a glass of sparkling water. Her bare feet were curled under her on the outdoor lounge and she still wore her black dress, the jersey soft and comfortable.

It was one she'd designed herself. She'd felt inordinate pride when Damon complimented her on her appearance.

Alkis had almost had an apoplexy at the idea of his spouse wearing anything 'home-made', no matter how exquisite. He couldn't see her creative flair, only the notion that anything she accomplished must be second-best.

As for starting her own home-wares and design boutique! He'd deemed it far beyond her limited female abilities.

Silently Callie lifted her glass in a silent toast.

To her new venture.

To being her own woman.

To no longer being classed as second-best.

'Sorry.' Damon's voice came from behind her, sending a shivery trail of awareness down her spine. 'It was an urgent call from California but it's sorted now.'

'That's all right.' Callie shrugged. 'I was enjoying the quiet.'

Without him. Was that the implication?

Damon frowned, wondering if she'd prefer to be alone.

He stepped into her line of vision, his heart contracting at the vision she presented. Her dress was simple and sexy, her hair up, emphasising the slender column of her throat, and she wore no jewellery. Yet her eyes were brighter than emeralds, her smile more alluring than pearls.

The flight of fancy should have made him scoff. A lifetime's experience had proved no woman, particularly an indulged woman from a privileged family, deserved to be put on a pedestal.

Yet Damon's cynicism foundered. He *knew* she was more than she'd seemed.

The time had come to unravel the secrets she hid.

'What are we toasting?' He raised his glass of wine.

Her lips curved in a secret smile that clenched his belly in a spasm of primitive ownership.

Sexually she was his.

But he wanted more. He was greedy for her in so many ways.

'New beginnings.' She touched her glass to his.

'To new beginnings.'

He sat with his back to the glow of the city lights. He'd seen that view many times. Tonight his focus was the enigmatic woman before him. He was determined to keep his distance until he had answers.

'Tell me why you married.'

Her head jerked and her eyes rounded.

'I don't talk about my marriage.' Frost coated her voice.

'I know. I want you to tell me anyway.'

'Why should I?' Her chin jutted.

'Why shouldn't you?' he countered, leaning forward, his elbows on his knees, his glass clasped in both hands. 'You're not protecting anyone, are you?'

'No,' she said after a moment's hesitation.

'Then what have you got to lose?'

'It's private.'

Ah, there it was, the serene expression of queenly disdain. It proved he was on dangerous ground. Instinct told him the secret of the real Callie lay buried in the circumstances of her marriage.

He didn't need to understand her to bed her.

He didn't need to understand her to revel in the heady bliss of the best sex of his life.

Yet still he needed to know.

Callie was more than the latest woman in his bed. Even that realisation couldn't deter him.

He didn't do serious relationships. But with Callie he needed more than a simple physical relationship. The knowledge had gnawed at him for weeks.

'You're afraid to tell me. Is that it?'

'Why should I pander to your curiosity?' Glittering eyes stabbed him. He watched her defences go up, just as they had in her uncle's home. Only he'd been too angry to see there was more to her attitude than pride and superficiality. That there was hurt as well.

This time he wouldn't react to the challenge. Though his body stirred at the idea of harnessing all the resentful energy quivering through her and directing it into passion that was hot and erotic and satisfying.

From the moment he'd found her huddled and grief-stricken on his yacht, the need to know more had grown. He'd felt her pain. There was so much more, unresolved. It had just taken him a while to realise it.

'Why are you scared?'

Predictably she met his gaze squarely. 'I'm not.'

'Don't you know what they say about sharing painful experiences so they don't fester and take over your life?'

Is that what had happened to Callie?

'We toasted new beginnings. You have to let the past go before you can make that new beginning.'

'Spare me your pop psychology.'

Yet her eyes narrowed, her mouth pursed, as if she considered the idea.

Silence stretched for long minutes, broken only by the distant hum of traffic. Damon watched her intently, alive for the slightest relaxation in her rigid posture.

'I'll tell you,' she said at last, looking stiffer than before. 'On one condition.'

He raised an eyebrow. 'Yes?'

'You answer a question of mine.'

'Done.' His reply was instantaneous.

He sat back, sipping his wine. Better not to crowd her. Yet his scrutiny was intense as he waited, watching her fiddle with the glass in her hand.

'I married for my family,' Callie said eventually, looking beyond him to the city.

'In what way for your family?'

'My uncle promoted the match. Alkis was an acquaintance of his.' Her voice was devoid of emotion. Eerily so.

'You married because your family thought it a good match?' He couldn't believe they'd consider a thirty-five-year age-gap wise.

'My uncle did.' She paused and gnawed her lip in the first overt sign of stress she'd revealed. Then the words poured out in a rush. 'The company was in financial difficulties. They were facing ruin. Uncle Aristides said that without Alkis' support the family would lose everything. But Alkis would only help if he could have me.'

'Your husband made you part of a *business* deal?' Damon's skin crawled at the notion. 'And Aristides agreed?'

The idea of her being given in marriage, a bonus to sweeten a contract, sent wrath surging through him. Acid burned his mouth and his fingers tightened around the glass. He'd like to tighten them around her uncle's flabby neck.

'Yes.'

'The bastards.' There was no question she was genuine. It was there in her anguished eyes and the tight curl of her lips. After living with her for weeks he knew this had the ring of truth. Far more believable, now he knew her, than her vamping an older man to win a fortune.

She was one of the least avaricious women he knew.

'You can say that again.'

'Your uncle bullied you into it.' It wasn't a question. He knew enough about Aristides Manolis to imagine how he'd threaten a young girl to get what he wanted.

'That's how he operates,' she murmured. 'My first love affair had ended badly and I was too wrapped up in that to put up much resistance. I felt I'd be responsible if my aunt and cousin ended up homeless.'

Curiosity about her lover sidetracked him until he realised the broader implications of her statement.

'Manolis just tried it again.' Damon put down his glass before he broke the stem; such was the fury rising within him. 'He tried to sell his daughter to sweeten our negotiations!'

Damon's fury exploded at the notion of being part of such a scheme, however unwittingly.

He'd dismissed the idea of such a match as wishful thinking by Manolis. Had Callie's cousin been under the same intimidating pressure to marry a wealthy man? It made Damon feel unclean.

'He wanted to force Angela too?'

She looked at him curiously. 'Of course.'

Damon leaned back, remembering Angela's diffidence, her nervousness. He'd put it down to natural timidity, but perhaps it was fear of failing to please him, or worse, fear that she'd have to marry him.

He catapulted to his feet, a tide of rage sweeping him along. How had he been so blind? He'd used Callie's protectiveness of her cousin to get her into bed, not for a moment realising the girls had genuine reason to take the idea of such a marriage seriously. That it had happened before.

He'd played on what he thought were Callie's unfounded fears and jealousies.

Christos! It must have been like history repeating itself for Callie, watching her uncle try to bring off another business coup by selling his daughter for profit.

He swung round. She looked calm in the moonlight, her face devoid of expression. Now he knew her he understood she concealed her pain. Pressure built in his chest, squeezing his lungs till his breath jettisoned in a rush.

He'd hurt her, unknowingly playing on what must be deep wounds from the past. He cringed inwardly at the accusations he'd made about her marriage. And the way he'd threatened so glibly to marry Angela if Callie didn't give herself to him.

'I'm sorry.' The words were such a strangled burr he had to repeat himself. 'I'm sorry, Callie. I had no idea. I was too busy finding fault and fighting lust to see what was in front of me.'

'You didn't know,' she said finally, shrugging, but she couldn't deceive him. The tense set of her shoulders, the line of her mouth belied her insouciance.

'I hurt you.' He stepped close, till she looked up and met his eyes. There at last he saw a flicker of something other than stoic control.

'I didn't see how serious Manolis was about his plan to marry me to Angela. Didn't realise the pressure he was applying to Angela. And to you.'

Callie scrutinised him as if she could read in his face whether he was genuine.

'You didn't deserve the way I treated you.' Understanding the full implications iced his bones. Never had he treated a woman so badly.

'No, I didn't.' She slumped back as if the fight had left her, or the effort of maintaining her composure was suddenly too much.

He sat beside her and took her limp hand in his.

'I behaved like an arrogant bastard too.'

Her lips curled in a lopsided smile that tore straight through him. 'You did. You were appalling.'

Yet she let him hold her hand between his palms without pushing him away.

'As bad as Alkis?' he couldn't help asking. Now he saw his actions in a new light. Circumstances and his own outrageous behaviour bracketed him together with the man he'd despised for pursuing a nubile young trophy wife.

His breath stopped as he awaited her answer. For whatever there was between them—sex, excitement, even a strange, raw relationship built on moments of connection like this—Damon wasn't ready to end it.

He wasn't ready to relinquish her.

'Nothing could be as bad as that.'

The quiet vehemence in her clipped words sliced through his thoughts. Her hand balled into a fist in his hold. What the hell?

'Why not?'

Glittering eyes focused on him. In the moonlight he saw brilliant tears well and cling to her lashes.

That curious tight feeling in his chest struck again and his hands tightened around hers.

'My husband was a manipulative, suspicious control freak. Mental cruelty was his speciality.' She drew a deep breath. 'I'm glad he's dead.'

Before Damon could respond she spoke again.

'I don't want to talk about him. But you owe me an answer.'

She halted, looking down at their linked hands then up again in a sidelong glance that told him she'd chosen her question carefully.

'Tell me. Who did the woman tonight remind you of?'

CHAPTER THIRTEEN

DAMON flinched at the abrupt change of subject. His grasp loosened, allowing her to slide her hand free.

He didn't want to talk about this.

It was too private, even now too raw.

He met her unwavering stare.

He owed her. He'd trampled through Callie's traumatic past, hauling to the surface long-buried pain and fear. Because he *had* to know what made her tick.

Now he understood. At least enough to piece together some of the betrayal and disappointment she'd suffered.

Six years with a man she didn't love or respect. With a man she abhorred. Yet she'd played the role of devoted spouse and affectionate niece rather, he guessed, than hurt the ones she loved: her aunt and cousin.

He heard enough snippets of phone conversations to know Callie rang them often, keeping tabs on her aunt's health.

Callie Manolis was the opposite of what he'd believed her. Strong, principled, stoic, with an integrity that shone.

Completely different from the woman she asked about.

Callie watched Damon withdraw as silence enclosed them.

For the first time she'd been honest about her marriage. Not even with Aunt Desma had she come clean about how awful it had been. Her aunt would have blamed herself for not stopping the wedding.

Callie's emotions were muddled. The old negative feelings surfaced. Yet she had a confused sense of something positive emerging from the morass of regret, anger and self-doubt.

It had taken all her strength to hold her own against Alkis' attempts to undermine her confidence. Damon's apology, so direct yet so obviously real, was like a brisk breeze, chasing away the tattered storm clouds of old pain.

Such a simple thing, an apology. But the first one Callie had received for any of the trauma inflicted by the men in her life.

It felt momentous.

Had he been right about sharing the past to make a fresh start?

Callie doubted it was so easy. But she felt better, as if some of the hurt she'd carried so long had healed.

And she felt...trust.

Damon wasn't the amoral opportunist she'd thought. He'd been shocked by her story.

She'd had glimpses of a man who might be far more, far better than the egotistic, power-hungry shark she'd thought him. Now she had proof.

Relief lightened her very bones. She was tied to Damon in deep, inexplicable ways, not just by sexual passion. For the first time she dared hope her feelings weren't self-destructive. That he was a man worth trusting.

He raked a hand through his hair, his face set in grim lines that told their own tale.

Instinct had been right. Some woman in his life had left her mark indelibly.

Did he trust Callie enough to share that secret?

Or had trust been a one-way street?

She held her breath as she waited for him to brush off her question with a glib reply.

'Leta Xanthis.' The words were a grating whisper. 'She reminded me of Leta Xanthis.'

'Leta...?' Callie frowned. The name was vaguely familiar.

'I forget. You didn't grow up in Greece.' His voice was terse.

'She was wife to the most powerful media mogul in Europe. Her beauty and glamour made her a household name.'

Callie nodded. 'She's dead, isn't she?'

'A drug overdose. It caused quite a stir.' Damon sounded as if he were reading a boring news item, not talking about someone he'd known.

Callie watched his mouth compress, his brows furrow. His hand speared again through his hair.

'Was she a friend of your family?'

He snorted. 'Hardly!' His head jerked back in obvious disgust and he shot to his feet. Energy sizzled through him as he paced to the railing on the edge of the terrace.

When he swung back his face was in shadow, the glow of city lights and the moon behind him.

'We didn't mix with the likes of her. She'd have been outraged.' He drew a slow breath. 'When my father died my mother supported us by cleaning houses for rich families with coastal villas.'

Callie heard the ripple of anger in his words. Damon was a proud man. It would have scored his pride to see his mother toiling for others in such a way.

'How old were you?'

'Seventeen. I'd dropped out of school and worked as a handyman and gardener on the same estates. But I didn't earn enough to support the family. My mother still had to endure years of grinding toil.'

Regret laced his tone. Obviously he'd felt he should have been able to step straight into his father's shoes and support the whole family.

'Leta Xanthis owned one of the villas?'

His head reared up as if Callie had interrupted deep thoughts.

'Her husband did. He rarely visited and she used it for entertaining.' He almost spat the last word, the venom in his voice so patent that Callie shivered, rubbing her hands over her arms.

'She knew your mother?'

'She wouldn't notice the woman who scrubbed the toilets or cleaned the filth after her orgies.'

Orgies? Surely he exaggerated.

'But she did notice the kid who came to trim the shrubs and look after the pool.' His words were bitter.

Callie sat up straight as his meaning sank in. 'She came on to you? When you were seventeen?' How much older had she been?

'Don't be so shocked.' Callie hated the world-weary cynicism of his tone. 'Leta came on to anything in trousers. She wasn't the only one. I learned early all about the carnal appetites of rich women with too much time on their hands.'

'She seduced you?' Callie choked on the words.

'No. But that only made it worse. I became a challenge. To her and her friends. What had become occasional visits to the villa grew more frequent, till finally she lost patience and found someone new to target.'

No wonder Damon had a low opinion of socialites. Even as a teenager he must have been breathtakingly handsome. If rich women had thrown themselves at him, it was no surprise he was jaded. Or that he didn't trust women who lived off wealthy husbands while amusing themselves with lovers.

Which was how he'd viewed her when he met her in her uncle's home.

The tension eased from Callie's shoulders as she realised his readiness to believe the worst didn't stem from anything she'd done but from a lifetime's mistrust.

Hadn't she felt the same repugnance at the shallow games played by Alkis' friends?

The sight of Damon turning to pace the length of the garden drew Callie to her feet. He was stiff with tension.

'Damon?' She took a step towards him then faltered as he slammed to a stop, one hand braced on a column supporting a pergola of scented flowers. Callie thought back to his last words and foreboding filtered through her.

'Who did Leta target instead?'

Even from here Callie saw the spasm rack his body before his unnatural stillness resumed. Whatever had happened, this wasn't easy for him.

No easier than her revisiting her time with Alkis.

'My sister.' The words bit like bullets from a machine gun. Callie's throat closed in horror.

'Sophie had come with me one afternoon while I made repairs. I needed another pair of hands and Sophie was always eager to help.' He paused, then continued in a rush.

'One of Leta's boyfriends saw her and wanted her. Leta wasn't above pandering to his whims. She got Sophie alone and invited her to a party that night. But it had to be a secret. Unfortunately my sister was in a rebellious phase and thrilled by the invite. She was sixteen and too innocent to know what to expect.'

Callie pressed a hand against her churning stomach. She wanted to tell Damon to stop, but the words stuck.

'We didn't realise she was missing till late. One of the younger girls woke and noticed she wasn't in bed.'

'You went looking for her?'

Of course he had. The role of protector was ingrained in him. She'd heard it in his voice as he described his family circumstances. Callie had experienced it first-hand on his yacht when he'd cared for a distraught woman.

'I was almost too late.' The words grated out. Instinctively Callie closed the gap between them, needing to offer comfort. She stopped within reach of his taut, looming frame. He radiated tension. She felt it shiver through her.

'What happened?'

'He'd drugged her, or maybe it was alcohol. Whatever, she was out of it, lying there with her pretty dress rucked up high and…'

Callie wrapped her arms around Damon's waist, holding him close. The thunder of his heartbeat against her ear and the sound of his raw breathing filled the night. He was wound so incredibly tight.

'He didn't see me till I smashed his face in.'

His muscles quivered beneath her hold, reliving the moment of violence. Satisfaction coloured his voice. Callie couldn't blame him. Her hands had clenched in sympathy.

He heaved a mighty sigh and she felt those muscles ease a fraction. 'I ran foul of Leta's other guests, who didn't like me leaving with the prettiest girl there. But eventually we got away.'

Callie tilted her head and saw him rub absently at the skewed line of his nose.

'That's how you broke your nose? Saving your sister?'

He looked down, his dark brows slanted, his eyes flashing with remembered fury.

'All that mattered was getting her out. A couple of black eyes and a bloody nose meant nothing.'

Callie shivered at the idea of a lone, teenaged Damon taking on a bunch of older men, primed by alcohol. It couldn't have been easy. It must have been downright dangerous.

She lifted her hand and stroked the sharp angle of his jaw, feeling the faint graze of stubble tickle her palm.

'What's that for?'

Callie shook her head and let her hand fall. 'Nothing.'

He was so matter-of-fact about saving his sister he wouldn't understand the sudden surge of sympathy and admiration that welled within her. The softening deep inside that made her want to cling to him.

Maybe only a woman who'd never had a protector could feel so choked up by the story of his rescue.

'What happened? Were they charged?'

'No. My mother thought a court case would traumatise Sophie. We were sacked and threatened with the law if we showed our faces on the premises.'

Indignation fired Callie's veins. 'That's outrageous! How could they threaten you?'

'It was their word against ours. Leta was wealthy and powerful. I found new work in a place where I could learn about making money and beating that type in the only way they understood—with even more wealth and power.'

'And Sophie? Is she all right?' Callie rested her head on his chest. His arms encircled her.

Warmth that had nothing to do with shared body heat and everything to do with emotional connection spread through her. Damon's acceptance, his honesty about his past meant so much.

'Sophie's fine. She's one of Athens' leading lawyers.' Pride vibrated through his voice. Callie heard his smile without seeing it.

'She lives here?'

'Most of my family live close.'

Yet Callie had never met them.

Because she, a Manolis, wasn't good enough? Or because she was only temporary? A knot worked in her stomach.

Then he moved and her train of thought dissolved. He slipped his hand through her hair, tugging her head back so she stared up into his fathomless eyes.

Something sparked between them. Something vivid and strong, like the erotic charge of passion they'd experienced from the start. But it was more. The echoes of their pasts, their raw emotions, the trust they'd shared, made this deeper and more powerful.

His gaze stripped her bare. As if he saw her naked, not her body, but herself. Callie Manolis, the woman who'd spent her adult life hiding behind carefully constructed defences, keeping the world at bay and herself safe from further harm.

She saw a man of honour, integrity and compassion. Impatient, quick to judge and eager to have his own way. But his honesty and caring made him unlike any man she'd known since her father.

Was it possible she'd found a decent man? Someone she could genuinely, wholeheartedly care for?

Callie had fought not to relinquish her barriers in the face of his steamroller tactics. But now she'd capitulated and instead of surrender this felt like victory.

Excitement blazed as his head lowered. His breath caressed her face, teasing her lips.

'Damon.' It was a cry of pure longing as her hands snaked up and dragged his head down.

The world lit to a blaze of glory as he claimed her lips, engulfed her being with his. He surrounded her, his arm a steel bar at her spine as he bent her back. Willingly she complied, trusting him to keep her from falling as he took her to heaven with his deep, drugging kiss.

Starbursts exploded as Callie gave herself up to ecstasy. There was no shame in surrender. Just acceptance.

Peace.

Pleasure.

For Callie had done what she'd never dreamed possible. With every last scintilla of hope and trust and courage within her, she'd fallen headlong in love with Damon Savakis.

CHAPTER FOURTEEN

CALLIE coiled her hair behind her head and pinned it. Soon Damon would be home and she wanted to look her best.

She grinned at the woman in the mirror. He'd appreciate how the scarlet fitted dress clung to her curves.

Callie revelled in the effect she had on him. No longer was she repulsed by the feel of hot male eyes on her. Not when that male was Damon.

She'd come a long way. From a wary, damaged victim hiding fear and pain behind a cold shell of detachment to a woman ready to trust a man. Enjoy being with a man.

A woman ready to embrace her future.

A future with Damon? Her pulse quickened. She hoped so.

Before him she'd given up trusting men. Yet he'd smashed her defences till she opened up to him.

How far their relationship had moved. They were bound by more than ties of physical desire. There was respect and caring as well as mutual delight.

For the first time in seven years Callie was happy.

Surely he reciprocated at least some of her feelings? Enough to build on? Increasingly he was interested in her, in her thoughts and plans, listening attentively as she described her first tentative steps into the commercial world. As if what she had to say mattered.

Did he have any idea what a balm that was? To feel as if she and her project was really important?

Callie had to keep reminding herself Damon bought and sold multimillion-euro businesses as easily as she designed an appliquéd hanging. Yet in these last few weeks he'd questioned and challenged her, almost as enthusiastic about her plans as she.

For the first time since she was eighteen the world seemed a rosy, promising place. With Damon beside her she felt capable of anything.

She, the girl who'd barely scraped a place at university, who'd struggled with her studies. Who'd been shown time and again her only value was decorative, or as a lever to financial gain. After years of Alkis' snide remarks and mind games, Callie felt free, capable, independent. This sense of power, of self-worth, was heady.

As heady as the joy of having Damon in her life.

The phone rang and she reached for it eagerly. It was probably Angela with an update on her wedding plans.

Only last week Uncle Aristides had stunned them by agreeing to Angela and Niko's marriage. Angela could have married without his blessing, but his threat to keep his wife from visiting their daughter's home once she was wed had stymied the idea. Now everything was turning out right.

'Angela?'

But instead she heard her lawyer's crisp tones. Excellent news, he said.

'Are you absolutely certain about this?' she asked after he explained his reason for calling.

'Absolutely. The manager of the new complex confirmed it in person. She said your venture is just the sort they want in their building. So much so that they're willing to offer a reduced rental for the first eighteen months.'

Callie rubbed her forehead. She might be inexperienced but even she knew that exclusive new retail complexes did *not* cut their rent for an untried business. She'd queried the rent, guessing it would be far beyond her capacity to pay, but unable to resist checking out the most desirable new location in the city.

'What sort of reduction are we talking about?'

The figure made her head spin. She groped for a chair and sank onto it. He described a peppercorn rental.

Callie drew a deep breath and tried to marshal her thoughts. 'There's a mistake. Why would they make such an offer?'

The silence on the other end of the line stretched out. When he spoke again the lawyer's voice was stiff, as if with embarrassment.

'I understand your current...relationship was a factor.'

'My relationship?' He could only mean Damon. 'I don't understand.'

'You do know that Savakis Enterprises owns the building?'

No. She hadn't known.

'And you think the manager is trying to curry favour with the CEO by giving his...girlfriend a special deal?' The notion seemed far-fetched.

Again that pause before answering. 'My understanding is that the offer was made on the CEO's instructions.'

Damon had ordered the manager of the most exclusive retail development in the city to lower the rent? She shook her head. He was interested and supportive, but he was, after all, a businessman. Why take on such a risk?

'Are you certain?'

'Absolutely.' He cleared his throat then paused. 'Kyrios Savakis has taken an interest in your affairs before. Given your relationship, I thought you were fully aware of that.'

'What sort of interest?'

'Your inheritance. You know there was some irregularity about accessing the funds your uncle managed.'

'I know all the circumstances.'

'Forgive me, but perhaps not all. The balance of your inheritance was topped up by Kyrios Savakis.'

What? Callie's head spun.

'Damon paid the money? Not my uncle? Are you positive?'

'Completely. I understand he was eager to rectify the loss. Technically the money came via your family's company, but the source was most definitely Kyrios Savakis. Of course, I didn't divulge your personal circumstances but he was remarkably well-informed. He wanted to set things straight.'

The phone shook as Callie's hand began to tremble.

Set things straight.

That was Damon's specialty, wasn't it?

She thanked her lawyer in an unsteady voice and hung up.

Damon had provided the inheritance her uncle had stolen. He'd gone to extreme lengths to help her establish her business in a place that almost guaranteed success.

Because he loved her?

She hiccoughed on a bubble of disbelieving laughter. No, not that. He cared for her, enjoyed intimacy with her, but he'd never spoken of anything long-term. It was she, so needy, who yearned for more.

He'd been furious when he learned of her past and guilt-ridden about the way he'd forced her into a relationship. She'd even wondered if his initial interest in her tiny business might be driven by the need to make up for his earlier attitude and show he wasn't like her husband.

Had remorse driven him?

Set things straight.

That was how they'd met. Because he needed to make her family pay for what it had done to his. Settling the score.

Was he setting things straight now because he felt guilty about forcing her to be his lover? He'd been stunned by the truth of her circumstances. He knew he'd hurt her, compounding the damage done by Alkis and her uncle.

She remembered Paulo's words about Damon needing to fix things. His strong sense of responsibility.

Did Damon see her as a victim who needed protection? A problem to be recified?

Her heart squeezed as the suspicion grew. Was that behind his interest and support that she'd so treasured?

Damon felt *sorry* for her?

In the mirror her face was stark white, her lips a slash of scarlet that no longer looked sexy or alluring. Her mouth looked like a clown's painted grimace.

She lifted her hand and wiped the lipstick off with the back of her hand. It smeared like blood across her cheek.

'Callie?' A surge of anticipation quickened Damon's step as he crossed the penthouse foyer. Energy sizzled through him, and, amazingly, a hint of nerves. He hadn't been this excited since his first business coup.

Today was another red-letter day. An even more important one, if the tumult of adrenalin in his bloodstream was any indication.

He patted the small package in his breast pocket, assuring himself of its safety.

Everything was arranged.

He'd contemplated an intimate dinner for two in his apartment. Then he'd decided tonight was an occasion to be celebrated more traditionally. He smiled, thinking of his siblings and their families gathering now at his mother's house, agog to hear his news. The scent of succulent home cooking would fill the air and the rich sound of laughter.

Callie would like that. And they would like her.

But first, a private celebratory toast. His housekeeper had assured him everything would be waiting as instructed.

He stepped into the sitting room and halted, his pulse revving as he saw the slim figure in red at the window, her back to him.

His heart crashed against his ribs then slowly took up a more normal pace. She did that to him every time.

Callie. *His woman.*

A burn of satisfaction warmed his belly. He was doing the right thing, there was no shred of doubt. His decision had been simple. She was the one he wanted.

His gaze swept the elegant room and he realised that without Callie it would be soulless and unbearably empty. Callie's presence made it a home.

He shook his head. He had it bad.

So bad he didn't even care!

Damon strode to the ice bucket that cradled a superb French vintage champagne. Swiftly he uncorked the bottle and poured the delicately hissing contents into waiting flutes.

Only then did she turn.

Damon smiled and held out a glass.

'Here you are, *glikia mou*.'

Glittering eyes met his. He saw her tension, felt the quiver of her fingers as she accepted the glass. She'd sensed tonight was important. Had she guessed how important?

His eyes swept her long dress, gleaming ruby fire in the lamp-light, tiny sparkles scintillating as she moved.

She'd dressed to please him. The knowledge pumped the blood faster in his arteries.

'You look gorgeous. Good enough to eat.' The rush of lust was inevitable. But for now he tamped it down. There'd be time later. All the time in the world.

His eyes rose to her face and he paused. Callie looked different. No lipstick. No glossy red to match her gown.

Because she knew he'd kiss it off? Damon eyed her lush pink mouth and realised he preferred her like this.

He took a step nearer, excitement building.

'Callie mou,' he murmured, his voice surprisingly husky.

He glanced at the wine in his glass, the tiny vibration on its surface betraying his unsteadiness.

Damon stood straighter, meeting her green stare with a smile that felt just a little ragged. He wasn't used to being anything except totally in control.

'We need to talk.'

'Yes.' She inclined her head fractionally and he was struck by her poise. How it contrasted with his sudden ridiculous anxiety.

He hadn't rehearsed what he'd say. He was a persuasive

speaker and he knew what he wanted. It hadn't entered his mind that finding the right words might be difficult. But then what practice had he at this? It was new territory.

'About the future.'

'Good.' Her lips pursed. He watched her heft a deep breath and his gaze strayed appreciatively to her breasts. His hands itched to reach for her. 'I wanted to talk to you too.'

She paused, her eyes skating away from his. 'I've decided to leave.'

Damon watched her lips move, heard the words but couldn't believe what he was hearing.

His heart lurched then began pounding triple time.

'I can't see the humour in your joke, Callie.'

She turned to stare out at the city lights, presenting her perfect profile. It looked carved out of cool marble.

'I'm not joking.' Her voice was a low whisper. She lifted her glass and drank. Not a delicate sip but a long draught, her throat working almost convulsively.

Blindly Damon reached to put his glass on a nearby table before it cracked under the pressure of his grip.

'You're not leaving.'

Women didn't leave him, ever. He'd always been the one to end relationships. But more. This was *Callie*. The woman he'd selected for his own. The woman he wanted in his life permanently.

Wanted? He *needed* her.

He paced closer then froze as she shrank away from him.

His spine crawled as she turned to face him and he saw the blind look in her eyes. She looked...shattered.

'Why? Because it doesn't suit your plans?' There was an edge to her voice he hadn't heard in months. Not since they'd developed a rapport, an understanding. A relationship.

What was going on?

'What's happened, Callie? What's wrong?'

'It's time to move on.' Her chin tilted higher. 'I don't belong here. It doesn't feel right.'

Feel right? It felt wonderful! She'd changed his life and he couldn't imagine it without her. Didn't want to try.

'I won't let you go.' The words shot out before he had time to consider them. He was functioning on raw gut instinct as he reached out and curled a hand round her slim waist. Nothing felt so right as holding Callie.

'I thought you'd given up threatening me.' The tiny hitch in her voice was like a blow to his belly.

'Callie! There's no threat. Don't you trust me?' He'd worked so hard to overcome the damage he'd done. Worked to build her trust in him after his earlier reprehensible actions. He thought they'd moved past that, even though guilt still scored him for the way he'd treated her.

Again she lifted her glass and swallowed. 'As much as I trust any man.'

Her words speared his conscience.

'Callie mou...' he sidled closer, slipping his arm round her '...you can trust me.'

Tension vibrated through her body.

'You're a good man, Damon. But I don't belong here. I don't belong with anyone. I prefer to live alone.'

'You don't mean that.' He took the glass from her hands and put it down. Then he wrapped his arms round her and pulled her stiff body towards him, revelling in her softness against him. 'We're good together, Callie. You know we are.'

'Sex.' She shrugged and turned her head to avoid his kiss. Instead his lips grazed her ear. Instinctively he bit gently on her lobe and felt her shiver in response.

'See how you respond to me?' Triumph stirred in his belly. 'You don't really want to live alone.'

'I'm tired of being your mistress, the woman who's not even good enough to meet your family. I'm one of the enemy, remember? A Manolis.'

'That's not true!' How had she got it so wrong? 'They don't think like that. I was the one intent on retribution, not them.

As for not being good enough, you couldn't be more wrong.'
He thought of his siblings gathering to welcome her.

'There just never seemed a right time…' His words petered
out as he realised she was right; he'd kept her from his family. At first because he didn't trust her, then out of habit. He
never paraded his short-term lovers before his mother. Then,
as he'd become more absorbed in his feelings for her, he was
too greedy to share her. He'd wanted Callie all to himself.

Until now, when he'd finally realised how important she was
to him. That she was the one woman he *would* introduce to his
mother.

Callie's hands pressed at his chest, trying to push him back.
But it was only as he saw her blink back tears that he relented
and stepped away. His arms dropped to his sides, empty without her.

'That doesn't matter,' she murmured, clearly lying. He felt
her hurt and cursed himself for his stupidity. 'What matters
is that I don't want to stay indefinitely till you feel I'm able to
stand on my own two feet.'

She wrapped her arms around herself as if cold. 'I'm quite
capable of looking after myself.'

'What are you talking about?' Frustration filled him and
the need to understand.

Her hair swirled round her as she shook her head, her face
growing animated. It blazed with an anger that made her eyes
shimmer jewel-bright. 'I'm not some charity case, Damon. I
realise your intentions are good but I don't need pity from any
man.'

'Pity? It's not pity I feel for you.' It was on the tip of his
tongue to blurt out exactly how he felt. But the look on her face
stopped him.

She wasn't ready to hear. Not yet. She still didn't trust him,
so why would she believe him?

* * *

Callie stared up at his wrinkled brow and the grim lines around his mouth. No. He really didn't understand. He'd only tried to help her. It wasn't his fault he didn't love her.

Suddenly her anger seeped away. She was tired. So very weary.

'I know how you interfered in my affairs.'

That stopped him in his tracks. His head reared back.

'I owe my inheritance to you.'

'You were entitled to it. And I could easily cover the sum.' He spread his hands in a gesture of openness.

He'd looked just the same all those weeks ago talking to Paulo about endowing a charity. He'd seen the need and he had the cash. Of course he'd step in to fix the problem. That was the sort of man he was. Generous and with an overactive instinct to protect. To set things right.

Except she wasn't a charity. She was a woman in love with a man who saw her as a problem to be fixed. The knowledge seared a hole in her chest, making it hard to breathe.

She didn't want Damon as a benefactor.

She wanted him as her equal.

'And the cheap rent in your new building?'

His gaze flickered. Obviously he hadn't expected her to find out about that. 'The place is perfect for you. It seemed a crime not to help you start up there.'

'But I have to do it *myself.* Don't you see that?'

If just once he'd say he'd acted out of love for her, because she was special, the woman for him...but that was wishful thinking. He'd acted to give her a new start after discovering the hurdles she had to overcome.

'You won't accept my help?' He drew himself up straighter, the distance suddenly yawning between them.

She shook her head. 'It's not about help.'

'So perhaps it's about control,' he murmured. 'You said your husband was a control freak. What exactly did he do?'

Callie frowned, not following his train of thought. 'I don't understand. That's not relevant.'

'Won't you tell me?' The sincerity in his voice, the tenderness in his eyes undid her resolve. Even now he cared. He wanted to remedy the past.

Whereas she wanted to forget the past and build a future.

Pity the only future she could visualise was a fantasy, with Damon by her side.

She sighed and Damon tensed at the pain on her face.

'Alkis always set limits. People I couldn't see, places I couldn't go. I lost count of the design classes and small business groups I joined only to find I had to withdraw. It was no longer convenient or we were taking an extended trip, or he was unwell and needed me. Always some excuse.'

'You could have gone anyway.'

She shook her head. 'He'd have found out and life would have been unbearable. He always knew where I was. Over dinner he'd quiz me about people I'd met that day, people who'd spoken to me.' She looked up and saw Damon's frown. 'He had me watched all the time, reports made on my movements. There wasn't a thing he didn't know about.'

Damon wished her husband wasn't dead so he could take him apart piece by piece. The damage Alkis had caused with his twisted desire for control was appalling. No wonder Callie was desperate to assert her independence.

What damage had Damon done?

Unwittingly he'd tapped into a vein of ingrained vulnerability. Nothing he did now could convince her he wasn't like her bastard husband. He'd tried to help but she thought he'd taken control of her life.

Damon swore under his breath, cursing his drive to act decisively. Should he have held back and consulted her?

He winced, knowing the answer.

'You think I'm like him.' He turned and paced the room.

He'd taken for granted Callie trusted him. More, that she reciprocated his feelings.

Had he pushed her so far he'd lost her for good?

'No! Of course you're not.'

But the misery was clear on her face, in the way she wrung her hands. Her pain belied her words.

He wanted to sweep her up and cosset her and caress her and make love to her till she forgot her pain. And he could. He knew even now that he could overcome her scruples and seduce her with his loving.

But the pleasure would only be temporary. Sooner or later she'd turn those sad eyes on him again.

'How can I prove you wrong?'

She frowned as if he spoke a foreign language.

'What can I do to make you trust me?'

'I trust you, Damon, I just…'

Don't love you?

Don't want you controlling my life?

Can't live with you?

Damon had never felt so helpless. So desperate.

'Then tell me what I can do. What will make a difference?'

He'd do anything. If there were dragons to slay he'd conquer them. He'd fight battles for her, overcome any obstacles. His only hope lay in proving to her he was the one man she could trust with her life.

Her mouth twisted and she shook her head.

'You can let me go.'

CHAPTER FIFTEEN

'THE new stock I mentioned has come in. Over on that wall.' Callie smiled at one of her best customers then moved away, letting the woman and her companion browse in peace.

It was almost the end of another long day and she was exhausted. Not from physical tiredness. She still got a thrill of pleasure from her work.

It was emotional strain that made her feel like a wrung-out rag.

Five months, three weeks and six days since she'd seen Damon.

With each day she grew more needy, hungrier for a glimpse of the man who'd dragged all her skeletons from where they hid in her cupboard, who'd made her face her greatest fears. The man who'd infuriated her and challenged her and disrupted her life.

Who'd supported her and listened to her and given her peace as well as pleasure.

The man she'd rejected because she was too proud to settle for anything less than his love. Because with him she'd finally convinced herself dreams might come true. And her dream was Damon—loving her.

Her heart plummeted. Now she had the independence and the opportunity she'd fought for so long. It was wonderful, satisfying and challenging. Proof that she *was* capable. That she was worth more than Alkis or anyone else, herself included, had thought possible.

But independence wasn't enough. Not now she'd had a taste of life with Damon.

She was greedy enough still to dream of what might have been. If only he'd loved her.

He must have cared for her a little, to go to so much trouble on her behalf. But being pitied and propped up was no life for her. To be cared for because he felt sorry for her—that would have destroyed her. Especially when he moved on to his next charity project.

Or worse, fell in love with another woman.

Callie tucked her hair behind her ears, blinking rapidly as she finished unpacking a consignment of lamps.

No, Damon didn't love her. He found her sexually compatible. She stirred his protective instincts. But in the end he hadn't tried to stop her leaving. That had hurt the most, the knowledge she'd been right, that what he felt for her was simply pity.

By now he'd have moved on. Found another lover. A man like Damon would never be short of female companionship.

Her teeth sank into her bottom lip in an attempt to stop a betraying wobble.

Callie avoided the news as much as possible, not wanting to see him with another woman on his arm. She wanted him to be happy but she couldn't bear the thought of him bestowing that special, bone-melting smile on someone else.

Her vision blurred.

'They're beautiful.' A warm voice behind Callie made her swing round, blinking hard.

A woman in her late fifties or early sixties beamed at Callie. Her dark eyes gleamed as she gestured to Callie's silk hangings on the back wall.

There were only two left of her series of seascapes. One day, when she had more leisure, she'd make some more. Her embroidery work had always been therapeutic, especially in the dark years of marriage when she'd had few outlets for her creativity and energy.

'I'm pleased you like them,' she murmured.

Truthfully Callie would be glad to see them go. Those seascapes held too many memories.

She'd begun them in the early days of widowhood: stormy scenes of lashing waves or foggy, deserted coastlines. She'd finished them in a burst of energy and happiness when she lived with Damon. In those the sea was clear and calm, the mood exultant.

Looking at them now, so vibrant and serene, Callie felt more than ever she lived in the shadows. Despite the thrill of her initial tentative business success, the joy was missing.

'My daughter tells me they're your work.'

'Your daughter?' Callie struggled to focus on the conversation.

'Yes.' The woman gestured to her elegant companion bending to examine a small bronze sculpture Callie had just put on display. 'She bought one a few weeks ago and I had to come and see the rest for myself.' Her smile widened. 'And the remarkable woman who made them.'

Callie remembered that hanging so well. Once upon a time she couldn't have imagined selling it. That scene reminded her of all she'd let slip through her fingers. Of the happiness that had shone so briefly. But in the end keeping it had been too painful.

'Thank you.' Callie wished she felt more enthusiasm for her work. She should be thrilled, but it was a struggle to summon the energy.

Yet the older woman's interest was genuine and Callie forced herself to focus.

'Would you like a closer look at them?' Together they walked towards the hangings.

'I sew myself, but nothing as beautiful as this,' her companion said. 'I can't believe what you've achieved with fabric and thread.'

'Why, thank you. What sort of sewing do you do, Kyria...?'

'Savakis.' Her dark, intelligent eyes took in Callie's instant reaction, watching calmly as she jolted to a stop, eyes widening. 'But please, call me Irini.'

Damon shot to his feet.

'She's where?' he barked into the intercom.

'In the foyer, Kyrie Savakis. Shall I tell Reception to send her up?'

'Yes. Straight away.'

Damon put the phone down, registering the bolt of electricity hot-wiring his body. His pulse leaped at the thought of Callie here. In his office.

His brain buzzed with possibilities. Why here? Why now? Thoughts crammed and jostled for consideration till he slammed a lid on them.

He sat back in his chair and propped his fingers under his chin.

Six months since Callie had run from him. Six torturous months in which he'd plumbed the depths of doubt, fear and despair. Letting her go had tested his resolve beyond bearing. Allowing her distance till she was ready to trust had almost killed him when his instinct had been to hold her close and prevent her leaving.

She'd left him no option but to stand helplessly and watch the woman he loved walk out of his life. That had gutted him, knowing he'd hurt her and there was nothing he could do to rectify the situation but wait and pray.

Today he'd reached the end of his endurance. He'd promised himself, after half a year of waiting, he'd visit her apartment this very evening. He'd given her enough time, surely, to deserve a second chance.

Why was she here?

His lips thinned. Whatever her intentions, what mattered was the outcome of their meeting.

There could only be one possible result.

The alternative, to continue life without her, was unthinkable.

He'd driven his staff, his friends and his family to their wits' end, pushing himself harder than ever, yet unable to stick to anything. He'd lost his enthusiasm for work, for socialising. Even for sailing.

He had to resolve this. Now.

'Enter.'

Callie stepped over the threshold of the massive doorway and halted, her heart leaping against her ribs.

Just as dark as she remembered. Just as virile and stunningly good-looking. If anything, Damon looked even better than before. Hungrily she devoured the sight of him.

With his sleeves rolled up, his top button undone and his tie missing, he looked as though he'd been working hard. His hair was slightly rumpled as if he'd dragged those long fingers back through it, as he'd once caressed her own locks.

Her thoughts juddered to a halt. Intimate images swirled before her and she had to shove them aside.

'Hello, Callie.' She couldn't read his voice, or his face, it was poker-blank. Unlike her own. She was sure her roiling emotions were visible for him to see.

'Hello, Damon.'

The door snicked shut behind her and she jumped, feeling the weight of tension bearing down on her.

'Won't you take a seat?'

'Thank you.' She stumbled forward, aware of him assessing every aspect of her appearance. She'd hurried here from the shop. Hadn't taken time to go home and change. Her clothes were neat but not glamorous. Suddenly she realised that after a long day her tailored jacket and skirt probably looked creased and tired.

Callie stiffened her spine and met his stare. Closer to him now, she noticed what she hadn't from the door—the lines of fatigue bracketing his mouth, the way his eyes seemed to have sunk a little as if from too little sleep. The grim cast of his solid jaw.

Her stupid heart pounded. He'd been working too hard.

But she wasn't in a position to remonstrate. She wasn't supposed to care.

Yet she did, so much it hurt.

'It was good of you to see me.' She hated her stilted voice, the need to hide behind social niceties and pretend she was calm when her stomach churned with nerves.

Damon inclined his head.

Did he deliberately try to make her uncomfortable, sitting on the other side of that vast desk, saying nothing?

It didn't matter. Her pride was sawdust and she didn't care. All that mattered was connecting with him again.

If he'd let her.

She'd thought today, when she met his mother, that there was a chance. Just a slim hope he felt something more for her than pity. The fact that he'd talked to his mother about her must mean something, surely? But, looking into his set face, she realised she'd come on a fool's errand.

Damon didn't love her.

Nerves stuck her tongue to the roof of her mouth for so long the silence thickened between them.

'Would you like some refreshments?'

'No. No, thank you.' She swiped her tongue over her dry lips as she tried to pull herself together.

'I came to apologise,' she said, meeting his direct gaze. 'I should have done it before but it took a long time for me to... sort things out.' She halted but he said nothing.

'I should at least have thanked you for your generosity in refunding what my uncle stole.'

He made a sudden, slashing gesture. 'Forget it. It was nothing.'

She leaned forward. 'No. You're wrong. It's meant everything. It's allowed me to make a new start. To prove to myself I'm capable of achieving something worthwhile.'

'And that's important to you?'

'Of course.'

He nodded, his mouth twisting in a lop-sided smile.

'And I wanted to tell you I'll arrange to start paying you back when—'

He shot to his feet. 'You'll do no such thing!' His voice reverberated through the still room.

For the first time Callie saw his eyes spark. She preferred him this way. Even furious was better than the distant aloofness she'd seen since she arrived. Her pulse quickened at the memory of Damon when roused.

'Is that why you came? To settle a debt?' Despite the glint in his eyes, his voice was cool.

Callie's insides nosedived. That was it, then. It had been a ridiculous, forlorn hope that absence would make the heart grow fonder. That Damon would realise it was love he felt for her, not sympathy.

Her throat closed on bitter salty tears she refused to shed. She groped for the bag at her shoulder.

It was over. Time to move on.

Perhaps one day years from now she'd remember what they'd once almost had without the terrible wrenching sense of loss. Fatigue dragged at her limbs and the familiar leaden weight settled on her shoulders.

'Is that all?'

Callie nodded, avoiding his eyes. 'Yes, that's all. Thank you for seeing me. I hope…I hope things work out well for you.' Hurriedly she stood and spun round towards the door, her eyes misting.

'Wait!'

Damon's voice pulled her up short. But it was the artwork on the wall before her that rooted her to the floor. Her eyes bulged as she took it in.

'Come and sit down again, Callie.'

Numbly she shook her head. She blinked but it was still there, a massive appliquéd scene directly opposite Damon's desk. Where he'd see it whenever he looked up.

Her knees began to tremble. Out of the corner of her eye she saw movement. Damon approaching. Yet she couldn't drag her eyes from the piece before her.

'You've got my picture.' Her voice was a reedy thread of sound.

'I have.' His voice was grave. She tore her gaze from the wall and tried to read the gleam in his midnight eyes.

Not just any picture. Her favourite. The one that meant so much to her she'd once planned never to part with it. The secluded, pine-fringed beach where they'd met.

'Having a glimpse of paradise between business meetings keeps me sane.' His mouth tugged up on one side, creating a deep, sexy groove in his cheek.

'It's not paradise.' Her voice was hoarse. 'It's—'

'I know exactly where it is.' He stepped close till he took up her whole vision. There was nothing but him. Callie breathed in the spice and man scent she'd missed for so long. Her eyelids flickered.

'That's why I asked my sister to get it for me.'

His gaze challenged. But it was all Callie could do to tamp down the rising bubble of excitement and disbelief inside her.

'That doesn't bother you?' he challenged. 'That you didn't know she was buying it for me?'

Callie shook her head, feeling a fizz of energy at the sudden glitter in his eyes.

'There's more,' he said. 'Not just that my sister told me about your work and I asked her to buy this piece.' His jaw firmed. 'You might as well know I asked her to visit your store in the first place. To see how you were.'

Warmth rose at the idea of Damon wanting to check on her. It took a moment to realise some of that warmth flowed from his grasp of her hands.

'Did you ask her to buy other things?' She tilted her head to one side, trying to read his expression even as her heart pounded a distracting rhythm.

'No. That was her idea. She was so enthusiastic she began telling her friends.'

'I've had a lot of word-of-mouth referrals.' But they were genuine, not orchestrated by Damon.

'You're not upset?'

'How could I be upset that you cared enough to look out for me?'

His whole body stilled, eyes narrowing.

'That's not all.' He looked so sombre her heart stuttered. 'I wanted to talk with you about it but you'd made it clear you didn't want anything to do with me.'

'What did you do?' She couldn't believe it was anything terrible but the look on his face worried her. She saw the white lines rim his firm lips, heard his clipped, distant tone and guilt speared her. She'd hurt him.

'I had words with your uncle.' A flash of satisfaction lit his expression. 'I persuaded him his interests would be best served by expanding his horizons. He's taken up an offer to manage one of my enterprises in the Caribbean. His wife isn't well enough to travel. She'll stay in Greece, preparing for your cousin's wedding.'

'That was your doing?' Astonishment filled her. Callie had spoken to her aunt just days ago. She sounded like a new woman, freed of Uncle Aristides' bullying influence. 'You've made a terrible mistake,' she blurted out. 'He'll ruin your business!'

The sudden rich rumble of Damon's laugh was like a blanket wrapping around her. 'Don't worry. His responsibilities aren't quite as broad as he first thought and he'll be strictly monitored. He might even have to work for a change.'

But behind the laughter Damon's expression was serious.

'You did that for me?' Callie could barely take it in. This was like a fantasy come true.

'And for Angela and your aunt.' He stood straighter. 'You'll say I was managing your lives.'

She shook her head. 'I think it's wonderful.'

'Truly?' His eyebrows arched. 'Even though you left me because I was like your husband, taking charge of your life?'

'No!' Callie reached out and put her hand on his arm. A surge of energy shot through her as she felt his living warmth. Her heart raced.

'You're nothing like Alkis!' The thought horrified her—that he'd believe such a thing. 'You're warm and generous and caring.' Her fingers clenched round his forearm, willing him to believe. 'You're...special.'

His penetrating gaze seared her.

'Then tell me, Callie, why did you walk out when I was about to ask you to marry me?'

Damon felt the spasm of shock rip through her taut body. Saw her eyes widen. In pleasure or pain?

His gut churned. Anxiety pulled every muscle and sinew tight. He'd given her six months to realise what they had together was special. Had he any hope at all?

'Don't, please.' Her jade eyes shone with distress and Damon felt a blow hammer his heart, robbing him of breath.

'You don't need to...' She looked away, the picture of misery.

Not as miserable as he'd be if he let her go again. It had nearly killed him the first time, even knowing he had to let her have her freedom if she was ever to return willingly.

'Don't need to what, Callie?'

She blinked and he touched a finger to her cheek, feeling the tears slide down her soft skin. His lungs contracted at the sight of her pain.

'Don't cry, *Callie mou*. Please.' It tore him apart to see her in pain.

'I know you feel sorry for me. But please—you can't marry me out of pity!' She hiccoughed and he wrapped his other hand around her, tugging her close.

It had been so long since he'd held her. Too long. His heart seized at the feel of her here, where she belonged.

'What are you talking about, *glikia mou*?'

'I...I...' Huge, tear-drenched eyes met his and, despite his confusion, he felt the inevitable spark of desire igniting.

'I've fallen in love with you,' she said in a rush. 'You must have realised that. But I can't bear to think of you staying with me out of pity.'

'You think I'd do that?'

She nodded, eyes overbright. 'Everything you did for me—I understand it wasn't personal. That it was altruistic, your need to right wrongs, but—'

'Altruistic be damned!' He hauled her even closer, wrapping his arms round her as if he'd never let her go. Impressing her body against his.

'That's why you left? You thought I felt *sorry* for you?'

She nodded against his chest and elation buoyed him as never before.

'The proposal still stands, Callie. I want you to marry me. I even have a ring to prove it.'

'Please, no. It wouldn't work. It—'

'Stop objecting for a moment, woman, and listen.'

She looked up then and he smiled. Damon's face felt as if it was cracking, so wide was his grin, so profound the relief that he sagged back against the desk, pulling her with him, off balance in his arms. Her warm, soft weight, all feminine curves and scented secrets, was like heaven after the purgatory of the last six months.

'I want to marry a woman who's deliciously sensuous, beautiful, talented, opinionated, determined. Someone I love.' It felt so good finally to say the words.

'Love!'

'Yes, love.' The weight of the past six months lifted off his shoulders in that moment.

'You love me?' Astonishment coloured her voice.

Damon spanned her waist with his hands and lifted her high, stepping away from the desk and swinging her round. She was light in his arms. As light as his heart. Her husky, surprised laughter floated all around him.

Who'd have thought happiness could be encompassed in one remarkable woman? He lowered her to the floor.

'I love you, Callie. I would be your husband, if you trust me not to run your life.'

'Really?'

'Really.'

'Damon.' She sounded choked up as tears flowed again. But he focused on her brilliant smile, knowing she cried from a joy that matched his. 'I trust you. I love you so much. I never want to be away from you again.'

The world stopped as he drank in her words.

Then Damon's primitive, possessive side urged him to seal the bond with more than a kiss. To take advantage of the long sofa against one wall and possess his woman instantly. It had been too long and he was so needy.

His arms tightened and he swung her off her feet.

'What are you doing?'

The feel of her in his arms was heady temptation.

'Taking you out before we get sidetracked,' said the civilised Damon who knew women enjoyed the trappings of romance. 'We'll celebrate with an intimate dinner for two after we collect your ring. And we'll call my family. It's time you met them.'

He strode for the door.

'I've met your family.' Her eyes glowed up at him in a way that made his heart hammer.

He jolted to a stop as her slender hand pressed against his chest. Her cheeks were flushed and her eyes slumberous.

'What I want now is you.'

Damon's heart filled as he looked down at her.

'I always knew you were my sort of woman, *glikia mou.* What a life we'll have together.'

* * * * *